Dear Otis,

Happy 8th Birthday!

With lots of love
from your Australian family
xxx

For Oliver, creative and inspiring – LC

For my Wild Australians – Ollie and Isla – CN

WILD
AUSTRALIAN
LIFE

LEONARD CRONIN

ILLUSTRATED BY CHRIS NIXON

ALLEN&UNWIN
SYDNEY · MELBOURNE · AUCKLAND · LONDON

INTRODUCTION

From the dazzling colours of shape-shifting octopuses to the towering clay cathedrals of tiny termites, Australia is a wildlife wonderland where the world's deadliest snakes live side by side with hopping mice and powerful kangaroos.

In this book you will encounter the fascinating and strange animals with which we share our continent, and learn how they live their lives and how they survive and flourish in some of the most challenging habitats on earth.

This book will help you explore and understand how every part of every animal is exquisitely adapted to work in harmony with the environment.

Wherever you open this book, you will embark on your own journey of discovery. You can begin with the Curious Discoveries pages where signs of the animals around us lead to other pages that reveal deeper insights into their lives. Or turn to any page you like and follow your own pathway, finding new revelations anywhere you visit.

Be curious, walk with your eyes wide open, and look carefully around you for the tracks and traces of Australia's hidden natural world.

CONTENTS

The Animal Kingdom 4
Classifying Living Things 5
Curious Discoveries 6
Magnificent Mammals 8
Skulls & Skeletons 10
Marine Mammals 12
Whales & Dolphins 14
Mysterious Monotremes 16
Surviving in the Desert 18
Creatures of the Night 20
Navigating by Sound 22
Perilous Predators 24
Spiderly Tactics 26
Devious Defences 28
Deadly Venomous 30
What Makes a Bird? 32
Feathers 34
Beaks & Feet 35
Taking to the Air 36
Dinosaur Bird 38
Thorny Devil 39
Radical Reptiles 40
Masters of Disguise 42
Metamorphosis 44
Fabulous Frogs 46
Incredible Insects 48
Dazzling Displays 50
Animal Architects 52
Cathedrals of Clay 54
Pond Life 55
Great Barrier Reef 56
Reef Dwellers 58
Blue-Ringed Octopus 59
Marvellous Marine Invertebrates ...60
Tree Life 62
Index 64

THE ANIMAL KINGDOM

FROM DELICATELY BEAUTIFUL CORALS to deadly reptiles and sea creatures that generate dazzling displays of electrifying colour, the diversity of Australia's animal life is astounding. More than one million different animal species live in Australia. They make their homes in every possible habitat, from the depths of the ocean to the tops of mountains and the harshest deserts.

The animals we are most familiar with are the **vertebrates** (animals with a backbone). They include all the mammals, reptiles, birds, fish and frogs, but by far the greatest number of animals belong to the **invertebrates** (animals without a backbone). Among them are the insects, worms, jellyfish, sponges, corals, molluscs and the amazing cephalopods (squid and octopuses).

INVERTEBRATES
Animals without a backbone

- Insect
- Worms
- Spider
- Jellyfish
- Sea cucumber
- Cone shell
- Sponges
- Coral
- Squid
- Crab
- Octopus
- Sea urchin

VERTEBRATES
Animals with a backbone

- Kangaroo
- Seal
- Frog
- Fish
- Dog
- Snake
- Turtle
- Bird

CLASSIFYING LIVING THINGS

KINGDOM
Animalia
Contains all the different types of animals

PHYLUM
Chordata
Contains all the animals with backbones (vertebrates)

CLASS
Mammalia
Contains all the vertebrates that are warm-blooded and suckle their young

ORDER
Marsupialia
A group of mammals whose offspring are born before they are fully developed and usually carried and suckled in a pouch

FAMILY
Macropodidae
Contains kangaroos, wallabies, pademelons, quokkas and their closest relatives.

GENUS
Macropus
Contains 14 living species: the kangaroos, wallabies and wallaroos

SPECIES
Macropus rufus
Contains just one species: the red kangaroo

To make sense of the incredible diversity of life, scientists have organised living things into groups according to how closely they are related to one another. The two major groups, plants and animals, make up most of the living things we are familiar with. All these forms of life are further divided into smaller and smaller groups, each with similar characteristics, finally arriving at a single species.

This science of classification is known as **taxonomy**, and helps scientists make sense of the millions of different life forms on our planet. This system also gives each species its own Latin name. Whereas an animal may have a number of common names, it has only one Latin name. The red kangaroo, plains kangaroo and blue flyer are the same animal: **Macropus rufus**.

Taking the red kangaroo as an example, this chart shows how the animal's physical characteristics determine its place in the classification system.

CURIOUS

Most Australian animals live secret lives – sleeping in their hideaways during the daylight hours, hiding in burrows, living beneath the water or blending into the background. But signs of them are all around us.

Footprints in the sand, a bleached skull, a discarded shell. These are some of the tracks and traces of our living world. They are clues that will lead us on a remarkable journey to discover the wonderful creatures that share our continent and the adaptations that allow them to live in perfect harmony with their environment.

🔍 Turn to the page numbers indicated to discover more about the found objects, tracks and traces shown here.

🔍 P.20
🔍 P.50
🔍 P.25
🔍 P.16
🔍 P.41
🔍 P.10
🔍 P.13
🔍 P.9

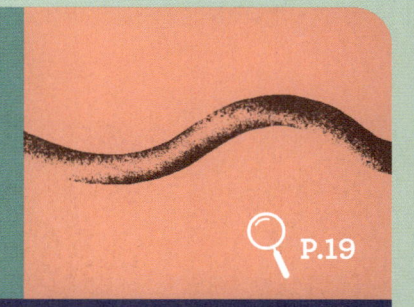

DISCOVERIES

P.29
P.19
P.56
P.43
P.53
P.48
P.44
P.32

MAGNIFICENT MAMMALS

KANGAROOS ARE MAMMALS, as are koalas, wombats, bats, possums, quolls, Tasmanian devils, dingos, Australian fur seals and of course humans. There are, in fact, around 5500 different mammals in the world, and Australia is home to 386.

Mammals have one characteristic that sets them apart from all the other animals: they feed their young on milk produced by the female's **mammary glands** – and this is where this group of animals gets its name from. The way young mammals develop divides the mammals into three different groups: the **monotremes**, the **marsupials** and the **placental mammals**.

MONOTREMES

The very first mammals that roamed the planet more than 180 million years ago actually laid eggs. They are called **monotremes**, and when their soft-shelled eggs hatch the tiny newborn feed on milk that oozes from pores on the mother's belly. Only five monotremes species exist today – the platypus and four species of echidna – and they live only in Australia and New Guinea.

PLACENTAL MAMMALS

By far the greatest number of mammals give birth to well-developed babies. These are nourished inside their mother's womb by a remarkable organ called the **placenta**; hence these are known as the **placental mammals**. Humans are placental mammals, as are bats, rodents and the dingo; so are dolphins, seals, whales and the dugong. Australia is, however, the only place in the world where the marsupials outnumber the placental mammals.

MARSUPIALS

Kangaroos, koalas, wombats, possums, planigales, dunnarts and quolls are all **marsupials**. Marsupial eggs develop inside the mother's womb (also called the **uterus**), but only for a few weeks. Baby marsupials are born without eyes or hind legs and are the size of a jellybean. Guided by the smell of milk, the newborn clambers through the mother's fur until it finds, and latches on to, her teats. Many marsupials have a flap of skin covering the teats that forms a warm, moist pouch called the **marsupium** (which gives this group its name). Here the young develop and grow until they are ready to explore the outside world.

Koala

Echidna

Tasmanian devil

Bilby

Wombat

Mammals come in a remarkable variety of shapes and sizes, and among the Australian mammals are the largest animal that ever lived on earth (the blue whale, which is as long as three buses, or one and a half times the size of the largest dinosaur that ever roamed the planet) and one of the smallest (a tiny, ferocious little creature that weighs no more than a 10-cent coin: the long-tailed planigale).

Spotted cuscus

Bat

Kangaroo

Striped possum

Dingo

Numbat

CURIOUS DISCOVERIES

Most Australian mammals like to hide from the heat in burrows or shady places, but for some, their footprints often give them away. These unmistakable prints show two long, powerful feet, and between them two rather delicate hand prints. They belong to Australia's most recognisable mammal: the red kangaroo.

Potoroo

Marsupial mole

Platypus

SKULLS & SKELETONS

ALL MAMMALS HAVE THE SAME basic arrangement of bones in their skeletons. What makes them look and behave so differently are changes to the size and position of these bones. The forelimbs of koalas are adapted for climbing trees, those of dolphins create flippers for moving through the water, while bats have extraordinarily long fingers and toes that support a membrane of thin skin enabling them to fly.

Long, chisel-shaped incisors for biting

Broad, flat cheek teeth (molars) for grinding

HERBIVORE SKULL

Grass is tough and very wearing on the cheek teeth, so the molars of most grazing animals keep on growing throughout the animal's life. Not so the kangaroos. They have four pairs of molars on each side of the jaw, but only the first pair grind the food. When these wear down to the roots they simply fall out and are replaced by the second pair. By the time the kangaroo is 15–20 years old it is down to its last pair of molar teeth, and doomed to eventually die from starvation.

CURIOUS DISCOVERIES

It's amazing what you can learn about a creature from a few bones. This long, pointed skull belonged to Australia's largest land mammal: the red kangaroo. And even if we knew nothing about this animal, the skull would tell us that the red kangaroo is a **grazing herbivore**. It has eyes in the sides of its head to look out for predators sneaking up while it is busy feeding. Those large chisel-shaped **incisor** teeth at front of the jaw cut through tough grass and shrubbery, while the broad, flat, cheek teeth (**molars**) crush and grind the foliage as the lower jaw moves up and down and side to side.

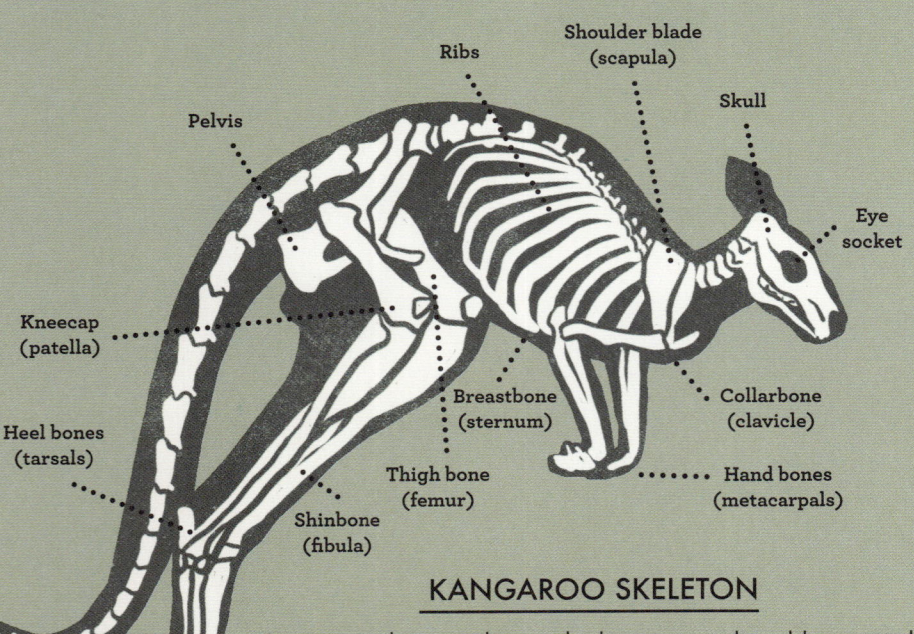

Pelvis
Ribs
Shoulder blade (scapula)
Skull
Eye socket
Kneecap (patella)
Breastbone (sternum)
Collarbone (clavicle)
Heel bones (tarsals)
Thigh bone (femur)
Hand bones (metacarpals)
Shinbone (fibula)
Foot bones (metatarsals)

KANGAROO SKELETON

Grazing in the open leaves the kangaroo vulnerable to attack by hunting animals. So this grass-eater needs to be able to move fast. Instead of running on all fours, kangaroos hop, and they hop stupendously. They have great big feet with amazingly long bones. The knee is close to the hip and this combination creates enormously powerful hind legs that can propel the kangaroo along at up to 60 kph, jumping fences 3 m high.

MODIFIED HANDS

Koala
Double thumbs for gripping trees

Dolphin
Long fingers and very short arm and wrist bones create a flipper

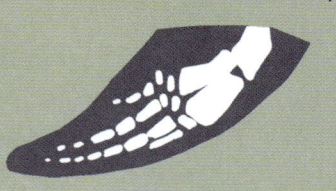

10

CARNIVORE SKULL

Meat-eaters (**carnivores**) such as quolls and Tasmanian devils usually have forward-facing eyes so that they can find and follow their prey. They also have small **incisor** teeth and very large **canine** teeth just behind them, used to grip and tear flesh from their prey. To crack bones and shred meat carnivores need powerful jaw muscles and sharp cheek teeth.

Large canines to grip and tear

Sharp cheek teeth for cracking bones and shredding meat

OMNIVORE SKULL

Omnivores (like us) have skulls and teeth suitable for chewing a wide range of plant and animal foods. They have sharp incisors to bite and tear, and well-developed cheek teeth to crush and grind their food.

Cheek teeth (molars) for chewing, crushing and grinding

Sharp incisors for biting and tearing

BAT SKELETON

Bats are the only mammals capable of true flight, and their whole body is adapted for this purpose. The bones are light and slender while their arms, legs and elongated finger bones provide a frame for the wing. Like birds they have powerful muscles to flap the wings, attached to a central raised bone on their sternum or breastbone, known as the **keel**.

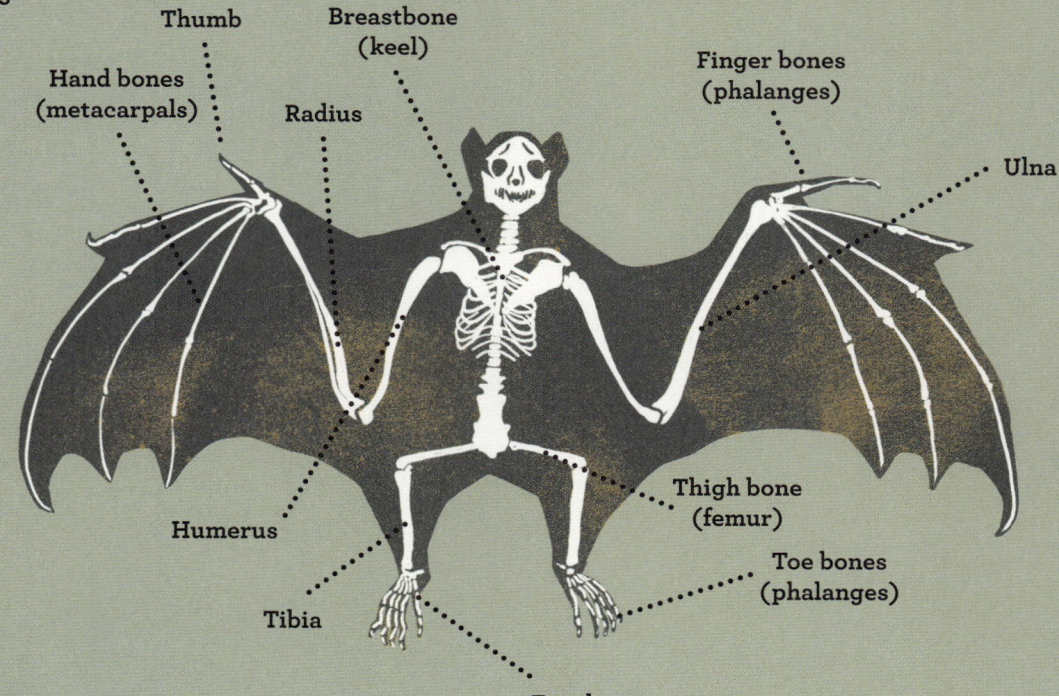

Thumb

Hand bones (metacarpals)

Radius

Breastbone (keel)

Finger bones (phalanges)

Ulna

Humerus

Thigh bone (femur)

Toe bones (phalanges)

Tibia

Feet bones (metatarsals)

MARINE MAMMALS

WHALES, DOLPHINS, DUGONGS, PORPOISES, seals and sea lions are all mammals, yet they spend most or all of their lives in the sea, and are known as marine mammals. Like all mammals they are warm-blooded, breathe air and suckle their young on milk. But their limbs have become flippers, their bodies are streamlined, and they can hold their breath underwater for up to an hour.

Dolphins surfing the waves, seals basking on rocks, whales breaching and blowing out to sea – it's not hard to spot some of Australia's marine mammals from our beaches and headlands.

Seal

Humpback whale

CURIOUS DISCOVERIES

You don't need to see sperm whales to know they are in our oceans. You may be the lucky beachcomber who comes across an incredibly valuable chunk of ambergris. This waxy substance, sought after by perfume makers, is more valuable than gold, and occasionally washes up on Australian beaches. Formed in the intestines of sperm whales from the beaks and other indigestible parts of the squid and cuttlefish they eat, large pieces of ambergris build up inside the whale and stay there until the whale dies.

Dolphin

Sea lion

Blue whale

Dugong

WHALES & DOLPHINS

HUMPBACK WHALE

The humpback whale is a smaller cousin of the blue whale and is often seen on its annual journey up and down the coast of Australia.

Humpback whales feed in the cold Antarctic waters and in spring they travel to Australia's tropics to give birth – a colossal journey of around 5000 km.

Humpback whale calves may be 5 m long at birth, and drink an incredible 600 litres of fatty milk each day (that's enough to fill six bathtubs!), pumped from the mother's huge mammary glands at the base of her pectoral fins.

Males communicate with other whales – sometimes several kilometres away – using deep moans, cries, yups and chirps, repeated and arranged into verses and choruses much like a human pop song. The song changes every year and each male sings its own variation of the song.

Baleen plates

FILTER FEEDERS

Although the blue whale is the biggest of all animals, it has no teeth. It feeds on tiny shrimp-like crustaceans known as **krill**, which are caught in the whale's gigantic mouth as it swims along. One gulp traps thousands of krill, and when the whale closes its mouth the water is forced through a curtain of bristly horny slats that hang from the top of the whale's jaw (**baleen plates**). The krill are trapped by the baleen plates and swept down the whale's throat by its massive tongue.

14

BOTTLENOSE DOLPHIN

Smart and playful, dolphins live all around the coast of Australia.

Dolphins are actually a type of whale, but unlike most other whales they have teeth and are known as **toothed whales.** Porpoises, killer whales and the mighty sperm whale are also toothed whales.

Toothed whales feed mostly on fish and squid captured with their sharp teeth. They also have very large brains and are believed to be some of the most intelligent mammals on earth.

Dolphins talk to each other using high-pitched clicks and whistles, and use **echolocation** to locate prey and find their way around in murky water.

Krill

BLUE WHALE

The blue whale is the largest animal the world has ever seen, and Australia's coast is one of the best places to find them.

A fully grown adult can be more than 33 m long and weigh 140 tonnes.

Perfectly streamlined and encased in a blanket of blubber up to 50 cm thick, this whale swims at up to 40 kph, propelled by massive tail flukes and guided by long, slender pectoral fins.

Blue whales roam the world's oceans, feeding in the Antarctic during summer when krill are plentiful. In winter they migrate north along Australia's coastline until they arrive in warm, tropical waters where they give birth.

Whales breathe through nostrils on the top of their head. Known as blowholes, they are kept tightly closed by strong muscles when the whale dives, and open when the whale surfaces, blasting a plume of air and water 10 m into the sky before the whale takes another breath.

MYSTERIOUS MONOTREMES

AUSTRALIA'S ECHIDNA AND ITS RELATIVE the platypus are so unusual that they have been given their very own subdivision within the entire class of mammals. They are the **monotremes**.

Part mammal and part reptile, monotremes are found only in Australia and New Guinea.

It's very hard to tell male and female monotremes apart, and when you look between their hind legs there's a big surprise – they have only one exit hole. Monotreme is, in fact, a polite way of saying 'one-holed' in Greek.

Birds and reptiles also have a single rear exit, known as a **cloaca**, which they use to get rid of their waste, to mate, and to lay their eggs. But monotremes have another surprise: they have an extra sense known as **electroreception** that enables them to detect tiny electrical signals produced by the nerves and muscles of the animals they like to eat.

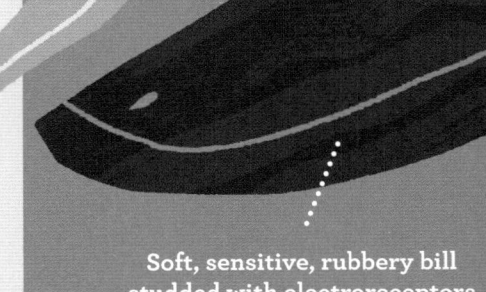

Soft, sensitive, rubbery bill studded with electroreceptors to detect prey

THE SUPER-SPINY ECHIDNA

The echidna is a rather lethargic animal and spends most of its time waddling around looking for a meal of termites, ants, earthworms and any other small creatures it can dig out of the soil or rotting logs.

Echidnas live in most parts of Australia and on the islands of Papua New Guinea. If you come across one it will probably flatten itself into a hastily dug pit, presenting a shield of impenetrable spines. Touch it and the echidna will dig itself further into the ground, keeping its more vulnerable underside well out of reach.

In most respects the echidna looks and behaves like a mammal. It has hair and feeds milk to its young. But this animal's extraordinary nature only becomes apparent when we examine the way the echidna reproduces.

This warm-blooded, milk-producing, hairy mammal is clearly not a reptile or a bird. It's a mammal with a **cloaca**. And if that were not strange enough, it also lays eggs.

Female echidnas lay just one egg directly into a shallow pouch just in front of the cloaca. The size of a small grape with a leathery shell, the egg sticks onto hairs in the pouch and hatches ten days later.

Like many baby birds and reptiles, the infant cuts its way out of the soft shell using a small tooth on the tip of its nose.

The newborn must find food if it is to keep growing. But unlike other mammals, monotremes have no nipples to latch on to. The tiny, blind, hairless echidna has to drag itself further into the pouch until it comes across a patch of hairs with rich white milk oozing from their bases.

The echidna also has lots of tiny organs called **electroreceptors** in its snout. When it pokes its long snout into the ground these organs detect minuscule electrical noises made by ants and termites, and the echidna licks them up with its sticky tongue.

THE VERY PECULIAR PLATYPUS

The extraordinary Australian platypus is the only other one-holed egg-laying mammal in the world.

This strange-looking creature appears to have the bill of a duck, the body of an otter and the tail of a beaver. When the first stuffed platypus was taken from Australia to England more than 200 years ago, people thought a trickster had sewn parts of these different animals together.

This sleek, streamlined diver feeds on small aquatic animals living in the murky depths of Australia's rivers and lakes. It has to shut its eyes and ears underwater to keep out mud and grit. Temporarily blind and deaf, the platypus finds its way around using a sensing device that is unique among mammals: its extraordinary rubbery bill.

The bill of the platypus is studded with thousands of sensory cells. Some detect objects by touch, while others, known as **electroreceptors**, detect the minute electrical signals made by its prey. The platypus waves its bill from side to side two or three times a second as it swims, scanning the muddy river bottom, snapping up shrimps, molluscs, insect larvae and other tasty creatures.

CURIOUS DISCOVERIES

Only one creature in Australia could have created this sharp spiny quill: the extraordinary echidna.

Similar to the quill of a feather, the spines of an echidna are made from the same tough material as hair, nails and claws (known as **keratin**), and are embedded in a dense coat of short fur that keeps the animal warm. Every few years the spines are replaced one by one to keep the defensive shield intact. Echidnas have little to fear from our native animals. Few are game enough to risk being stabbed by these needle-like spines.

Small eyes and ears in a long muscular groove that closes when the platypus dives

Dense, water-repelling fur

As many as 500 sharp spines cover the body, creating a spiky armour.

Round body covered in fur to keep it warm in very cold places.

Venomous spur on male's ankle used to keep other males away

Clawed, webbed feet for swimming and burrowing

Long claws on the hindfeet for grooming.

Spade-like claws on the forefeet for digging.

Long, beak-like snout with a tiny mouth and long sticky tongue.

Electroreceptors in the skin of the snout help to locate prey.

Paddle-shaped tail

SURVIVING IN THE DESERT

LIVING IN THE DESERT is the ultimate challenge for life in Australia. Water is scarce, and droughts can last for years. And when it does rain, it often pours down. Summer temperatures can soar to 50°C, and winter nights can be freezing cold. Yet our deserts are home to a great variety of wildlife, even water-loving animals such as fish and frogs.

You may ask yourself why they live there at all. It's not difficult to survive in the desert if you have the right adaptations, and there is much less competition from other animals. Some animals cope by travelling long distances to find food and water. Some creatures may never drink in their entire lives, extracting enough water from the food they eat.

Others bury themselves underground, emerging at night or just waiting for rain, slowing down their heart and breathing rates, entering an inactive state known as dormancy. Dormant animals can survive for months or even years without eating or drinking.

① WATER-HOLDING FROG

This frog has learned to live in arid areas by burying itself underground until it rains. When waterholes begin to dry up it drinks as much as possible and stores the water in its bladder and in pouches under its skin. Then it digs a burrow about 1 m deep with a small nest chamber at the bottom. Here the frog sheds its outermost layers of skin to create a waterproof cocoon around itself, and becomes dormant. It can live for years like this, slowing down its body processes, living on its body fat and stored water. The kiss of rain penetrating the nest chamber awakens the dormant frog, and after snacking on its cocoon the hungry and thirsty frog tunnels its way back to the surface to drink, feed and breed.

② THORNY DEVIL

This fearsome-looking reptile eats nothing more than black ants. They contain enough food and water for it to survive even severe droughts, but it can also obtain water by burying itself in sand dampened by the early morning dew. Tiny channels between the lizard's scales create a network of miniature drinking straws that draw moisture from the sand by capillary action and deliver it to the corners of the lizard's mouth.

③ SHIELD SHRIMP

Large numbers of these small desert shrimps appear in temporary pools 2–3 days after a downpour. They gorge on tiny microorganisms in the muddy water, and just before the pools dry up they lay millions of eggs in the mud. The eggs can survive for up to 7 years, awaiting the next downpour, when they suddenly burst into life, hatching into miniature shrimps.

CURIOUS DISCOVERIES

Deserts occupy more than one-third of the Australian continent. They may seem like pretty lifeless places, but take a look around and you will find the tracks of all sorts of animals in the sand: the tails of lizards create long curved impressions, often interspersed with tiny footprints; there may be the footprints of birds, dingoes or kangaroos; and intriguing holes leading to underground burrows.

4 SPINIFEX HOPPING MOUSE
The seeds these little marsupials eat provide them with enough food and water to survive even the harshest conditions. They never need to drink, and conserve water by huddling together during the day in a deep, moist burrow. They also produce urine that is almost solid, and collect water vapour that forms in their nostrils when their moist breath cools as they breathe out.

5 BUDGERIGAR
Flocks of budgerigars scour the deserts searching for food and water. They avoid the heat and conserve moisture by sheltering quietly in tree hollows and bushes during the day. If water is not available they lap up dew and roll in damp grass. But when conditions become too harsh they migrate to more favourable areas, flying hundreds of kilometres, often following thunderstorms. Budgerigars only breed after good rainfall when there is enough food to feed their young.

6 BLACK-FOOTED ROCK WALLABY
During the hottest part of the day these wallabies shelter in caves and crevices where the air is cool and moist, reducing the amount of water lost by evaporation. Another way they save water is by producing very little urine. All the water they need comes from the grasses, leaves and fruit they eat. Free water is only needed when food is hard to find.

CREATURES

CURIOUS DISCOVERIES

V-shaped marks like these on the trunks of eucalypt trees are made by the yellow-bellied glider, one of Australia's six gliding marsupials. This chatty and sociable little animal has developed a way of extracting sweet sap from eucalypt trees by biting into the bark until the sap comes oozing out, leaving behind these characteristic marks.

OF THE NIGHT

TO AVOID THE SUMMER HEAT and conserve precious water, many Australian animals are **nocturnal** – they hide in a cool, secluded place during the day and emerge at night or in the twilight hours to feed and socialise. It can be hard to spot nocturnal creatures. You can sometimes see their eyes shining in the dark, or hear the noisy grunts of koalas and possums.

1 POSSUMS AND GLIDERS
Sugar glider families live in large hollows in tall, ancient eucalypt trees and spend the daylight hours sleeping and chattering away. Like all our possums, they are strictly nocturnal and have very large eyes to collect as much light as possible.

2 OWLS
Owls have exceptionally large eyes able to detect even the smallest amount of light. Their dish-shaped face directs sounds towards the ears, which are at slightly different heights. This helps the owl to pinpoint movement even in complete darkness.

3 SNAKES
Although snakes have good eyesight, they use their forked tongue to 'taste' the air and pick up the scent of prey. Snakes can also feel the tiny vibrations made by animals moving around. Some nocturnal snakes are able to hunt in the dark by detecting the heat given off by warm-blooded animals. These snakes have special heat-sensitive organs on each side of their head.

4 INSECTS
Moths are super-sensitive to smells. Females attract a mate by sending out alluring chemicals called **pheromones**. Males don't need eyes to find a mate. Their feathery antennae are able to detect these pheromones and home in on a female who may be 10 km away.

EYES OF MANY KINDS

The amount of light entering the eye is controlled by the pupil. In bright light the pupil becomes very small, but in darkness it opens as wide as possible to let more light into the eye.

The closed pupil is usually round, but in some animals it is a vertical or horizontal slit.

Many nocturnal mammals, such as the yellow-bellied glider, have a mirror-like surface at the back of their eyes called the **tapetum lucidum**. The extra light reflecting back through the eye allows them to see in very dim conditions, and causes their eyes to shine red or white in the beam of a torch.

Insects' eyes are made up of many tiny tubes called **ommatidia**, each with a small lens to concentrate and focus the light. For this reason they are known as **compound eyes**. Moths and other nocturnal insects have huge eyes with thousands of ommatidia.

Sugar glider

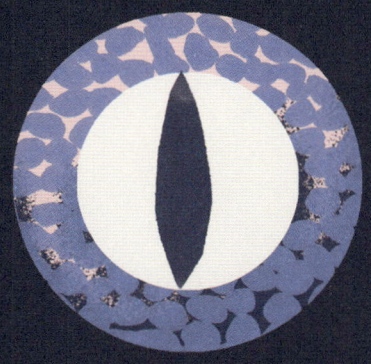

Snake

Owl

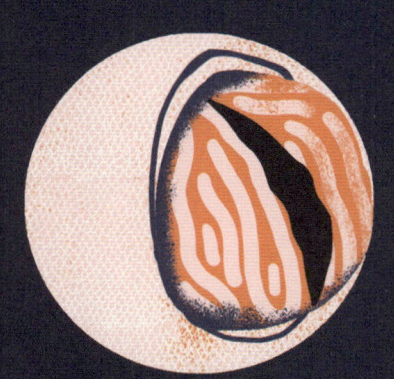

Gecko

Insect

NAVIGATING BY SOUND

EVEN IN COMPLETE DARKNESS, some animals are able to find their way around by listening to the echoes of sounds bouncing off the objects around them.

Winging their way in the dead of night through Australia's forests and woodlands, plucking mosquitoes, moths and other nocturnal insects from the air, bats seem to possess mysterious powers. Despite their excellent eyesight, small insect-eating bats use their acute sense of hearing to find their way around, avoid obstacles and catch their prey.

This amazing ability is known as **echolocation**. The idea is pretty simple: make short bursts of very high-pitched sounds and listen for their echoes as they bounce back from nearby objects.

Using nothing more than echolocation, bats can detect an object as fine as a human hair and hunt down tiny insects while flying at astonishing speed through the treetops, deftly avoiding collisions with branches and leaves.

Sound waves are emitted by the bat.

Sound waves are reflected from the insect.

Large, mobile, super-sensitive ears detect echoing sounds.

Folds of skin on the nose direct and focus the beam of sound.

WHALE ECHOLOCATING FISH

Dolphins, porpoises, killer whales and sperm whales emit sounds from their foreheads and use echolocation to 'see' the world around them in dark and murky water.

PERILOUS PREDATORS

FROM INSECT-EATING BATS to night-prowling quolls, Tasmanian devils and enormous whales, predators are lurking on land and in sea in and around our continent. While many predators rely on speed, agility and stealth to catch their prey, others blend invisibly into the background or use ingenious tactics to entice their victims to come within range of their deadly jaws.

BOX JELLYFISH

Propelled by jets of water, this deadly jellyfish uses its powerful venom to instantly stun or kill fish, shrimp and other sea creatures that come into contact with its stinging tentacles. Each side of the bell has a cluster of eyes that may be used to detect and move towards its prey.

DOLPHINS

Dolphins are intelligent and social animals that live in groups called pods, and hunt cooperatively. There are 15 Australian species living all around our coastline in bays, coastal inlets and offshore waters. Dolphins seek out schools of fish, surround them and herd them into an ever-tightening circle until they are packed as close as possible. The dolphins take turns to swim through the school of fish grabbing as many as they can while the others circle around to keep them together. Dolphin pods also corral fish by chasing them into shallow waters where they cannot escape.

ARCHER FISH

Swimming just below the surface in the rivers and estuaries of northern Australia, these small fish are on the lookout for insects resting on the riverbank or hovering above the water. Once an insect is spotted, the archer fish shoots them down with drops of water fired in rapid succession from its mouth. They seldom miss, hitting prey up to 2 m above the surface.

ANGLER FISH

Lurking among coral reefs, changing colour to match the surroundings, this bizarre fish has a long, thin spine protruding from head, tipped with a glowing, worm-like growth known as the esca. When other fish are drawn to this swaying lure, the angler fish opens its cavernous mouth and swallows its victim.

DINGO

The dingo is Australia's very own species of dog, and like the wolf it has different hunting strategies depending on the size of its prey. Small animals like rabbits, birds or reptiles are taken by solitary hunters, but when hunting bigger game, dingoes cooperate in packs. The size of the pack depends on the type of prey. Large packs collaborate to hunt kangaroos and occasionally sick or injured young cattle, water buffalo and horses. Lead dingoes chase their quarry into the path of other pack members who exhaust and bring down their victim, repeatedly biting until the animal collapses.

ESTUARINE CROCODILE

Australia is home to some of the deadliest predators on Earth. The 6 m long estuarine crocodile that stalks Australia's tropical coastline is the world's largest and most fearsome reptile.

INLAND TAIPAN

This most deadly of all venomous snakes lives in Australia's central deserts and hunts in cracks and burrows for mice, rats and other small mammals. Prey is usually cornered and bitten several times in quick succession. The venom acts so fast that the snake is able to keep hold of its prey without being injured.

CURIOUS DISCOVERIES

This cast-off spider skin is easily mistaken for a living huntsman spider. With a leg-span of up to 16 cm, this is one of Australia's largest spiders, and to grow it must shed its hard exoskeleton. The huntsman is a fast and dangerous predator, using its stealth and speed to catch insects, small lizards and even frogs.

25

SPIDERLY TACTICS

ARMED WITH VENOM-DISPENSING FANGS, an impressive arsenal of traps and lightning-fast reflexes, spiders are some of nature's most ingenious predators. Equipped with special silk-creating glands and tiny organs called spinnerets that squirt out freshly made strands of incredibly strong silk, spiders construct intricate webs to trap flying insects – but some Australian spiders have developed even more remarkable ways to catch their prey.

GOLDEN ORB WEAVERS

Golden orb weavers create complex webs up to 1.5 m in diameter. These spiders use the wind to blow a single, exceptionally strong thread from one branch to another. Once this bridge is created, the spider sets to work constructing a large circular web. Sticky threads trap passing insects while non-sticky silken pathways allow the spider to travel easily around the web. The spider sits patiently in the centre of her trap awaiting the vibrations of struggling insects.

NET-CASTING SPIDERS

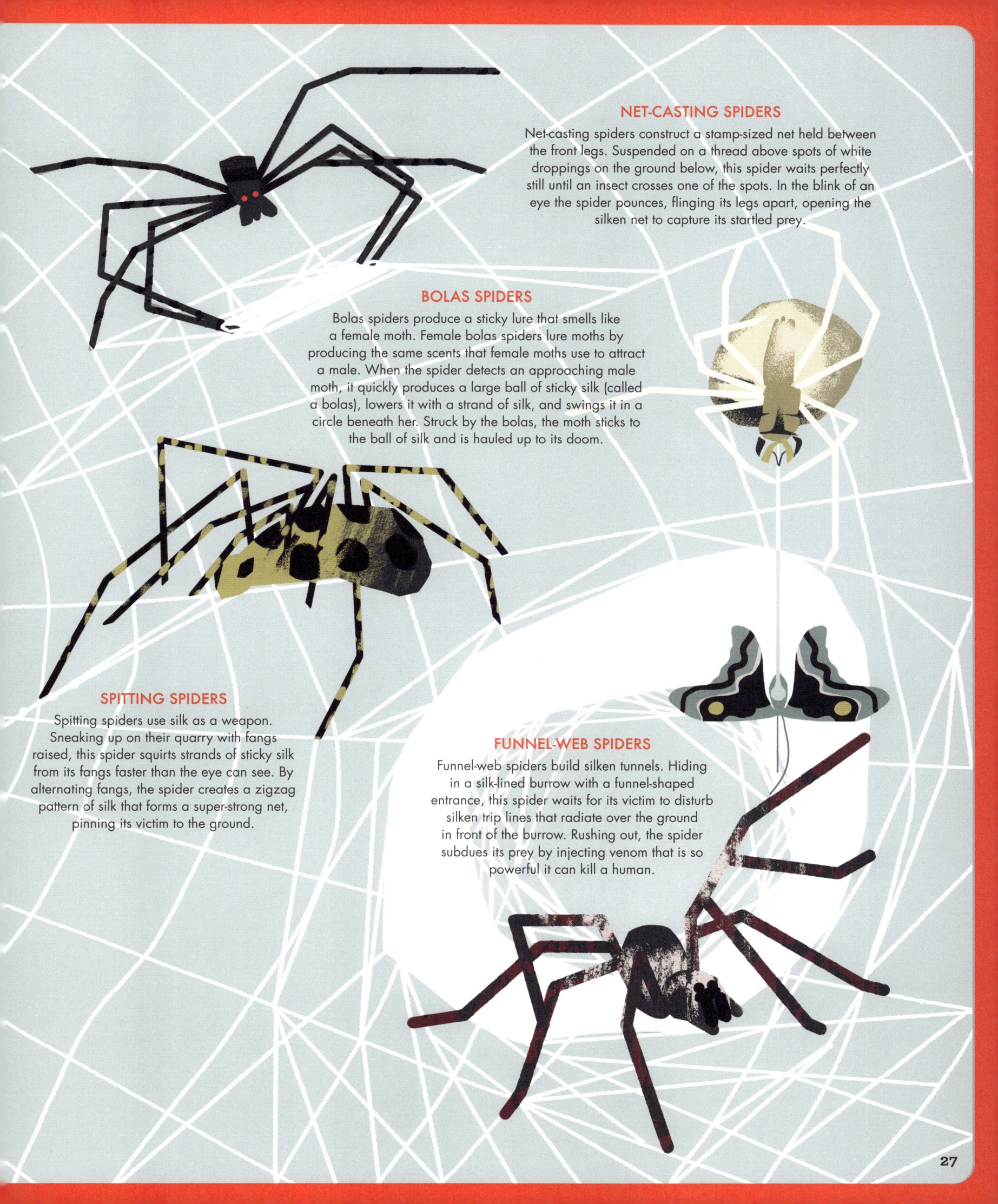

Net-casting spiders construct a stamp-sized net held between the front legs. Suspended on a thread above spots of white droppings on the ground below, this spider waits perfectly still until an insect crosses one of the spots. In the blink of an eye the spider pounces, flinging its legs apart, opening the silken net to capture its startled prey.

BOLAS SPIDERS

Bolas spiders produce a sticky lure that smells like a female moth. Female bolas spiders lure moths by producing the same scents that female moths use to attract a male. When the spider detects an approaching male moth, it quickly produces a large ball of sticky silk (called a bolas), lowers it with a strand of silk, and swings it in a circle beneath her. Struck by the bolas, the moth sticks to the ball of silk and is hauled up to its doom.

SPITTING SPIDERS

Spitting spiders use silk as a weapon. Sneaking up on their quarry with fangs raised, this spider squirts strands of sticky silk from its fangs faster than the eye can see. By alternating fangs, the spider creates a zigzag pattern of silk that forms a super-strong net, pinning its victim to the ground.

FUNNEL-WEB SPIDERS

Funnel-web spiders build silken tunnels. Hiding in a silk-lined burrow with a funnel-shaped entrance, this spider waits for its victim to disturb silken trip lines that radiate over the ground in front of the burrow. Rushing out, the spider subdues its prey by injecting venom that is so powerful it can kill a human.

DEVIOUS DEFENCES

PREDATORS ARE EVERYWHERE,
and Australian animals have come up with some
incredible ways to avoid being eaten.

① MANTIS SHRIMP'S SONIC PUNCH
This colourful crustacean packs a punch that can shatter aquarium glass. When threatened, it strikes out at incredible speed with a pair of heavy clubs at the ends of hinged arms. The speed and force of the blows produces enough energy to super-heat water in front of the clubs, creating powerful shockwaves that can smash the shell of another crustacean.

② SQUIRTING GECKO
That golden stripe along the golden-tailed gecko's tail is a warning sign to would-be attackers telling them to keep their distance. If it is attacked, however, this amazing little lizard has a very unusual way of defending itself: it raises its tail and sprays the attacker with jets of foul-smelling sticky liquid squirted from pores spaced along the top of its tail.

③ EXPLOSIVE BEETLE
When the terrifying bombardier beetle from eastern Australia is attacked, it blasts a jet of boiling hot, foul-smelling, corrosive chemicals from its rear end. It does this by mixing two chemicals together in a thick-walled chamber at the tip of its abdomen. The chemicals explode with a loud pop, creating a high-pressure spray of burning fluid. The beetle can fire the spray over and over again for up to four minutes.

CURIOUS DISCOVERIES

If you were to follow these tracks through the dry woodlands of southern or central Queensland, you may come across their creator, the beautiful golden-tailed gecko.

4 PLOVER FAKES A BROKEN WING

Plovers nest on the ground where their eggs and chicks make a tasty meal for hungry lizards, ravens, hawks and other animals. Plovers distract predators who come anywhere near their nest by limping and dragging one wing on the ground as if it is broken. When attacked, the plover miraculously takes to the air – leaving behind a surprised and confused foe.

5 TAIL-DROPPING LIZARD

Some lizards sacrifice their tail when attacked. By twitching certain tail muscles, the tail falls apart along a weak point. The dropped tail thrashes about, distracting the predator and giving the lizard time to escape. The lizard eventually grows a new tail – in fact, sometimes they grow two or three tails by mistake.

6 FISH THAT FLY

When attacked, flying fish use their fins as wings, leaping out of the water and gliding for 200 m or more to escape.

7 BOXING CRABS

Tiny boxer crabs (only 25 mm wide) use sea anemones to protect themselves. The tentacles of sea anemones are covered in stinging cells, and boxer crabs carry them in their front claws, waving them around like pom-poms to keep aggressors at bay.

1. GEOGRAPHER CONE SNAIL
One sting from this predatory snail can paralyse and kill a human in five minutes. Most people get stung by collecting cone snails from ocean reefs or by stepping on them. The venom is delivered by a tiny barbed harpoon fired at 650 kph from the cone snail's long snout. Stings are sometimes painless, so the victim may be unaware of being stung.

2. BOX JELLYFISH
One of the most venomous marine creatures known, the box jellyfish can kill a healthy adult in minutes. Venom is delivered by millions of tiny, harpoon-like stinging cells lining up to 60 tentacles hanging from the corners of the body bell. The pain of being stung is excruciating.

3. STONEFISH
Two stonefish species occur in Australia, mainly in the tropics. The spines on the fish's back contain venom that is among the most potent of any fish, and can be fatal to humans. Excellently camouflaged, these ambush predators hide on the sea bed and await their prey. They grow to about 35 cm and rarely swim away if disturbed. Their spines can pierce rubber-soled shoes, and most people are stung by accidentally stepping on them.

4. STINGRAY
Generally gentle and docile, stingrays will only attack if threatened by someone swimming above them or if they are stepped on. They strike with their slender tail, armed with one or more barbed stinging spines that inject a very painful venom. Although the venom is not usually deadly, the spines may pierce the heart or other vital organs.

5. COMMON LIONFISH
Lionfish rely on camouflage and lightning-fast reflexes to capture prey, but they also have extremely venomous fin spines. The venom is used for defence and is rarely deadly to humans, but stings are extremely painful and can cause paralysis.

6. INLAND TAIPAN
The venom of the inland taipan is the most deadly of all snake venoms. An average bite contains enough venom to kill 30 people, and can lead to

VENOMOUS ANIMALS DELIVER poisonous chemicals through their bites and stings.

- How do you capture your prey if it is faster, bigger or stronger than you? One very clever strategy is to create fast-acting, poisonous chemicals — known as venom — and inject them into your prey by biting or stinging.
- Venomous animals include spiders, insects, reptiles, frogs, fish, a multitude of other marine animals, and even a handful of mammals.
- Australia has more animals with deadly venom than anywhere in the world. Australia's box jellyfish, cone snail, blue-ringed octopus and stonefish are among the world's top 10 most venomous animals. Australia also has 20 of the 25 most venomous snakes on earth, including the world's deadliest snake, the inland taipan.
- Venom helps animals fight off predators, capture prey and deter competitors, but venom requires a lot of biological energy to produce. A scorpion, for example, takes around four days to replenish its venom after an attack, and during this period it has little energy left to move around and defend itself.
- Venom is a complex chemical cocktail made up of many different components. Cone shell venom, for example, contains more than 100 different substances. Some cause the nervous system to shut down or go into overdrive, while others destroy muscles. Snake venom may cause the blood to clot or lead to unstoppable bleeding, and venom from the stonefish causes excruciating pain.
- Fortunately, antivenom is readily available, and there are fewer than 20 deaths each year from venomous creatures in Australia.

death within 45 minutes. Fortunately, this snake lives in Australia's arid interior, and people rarely meet it in the wild.

7 EASTERN BROWN SNAKE
The brown snake is the second-most venomous land snake in the world and responsible for more deaths in Australia than any other snake. Much more nervous than the inland taipan, and more likely to strike, brown snakes are widely distributed and often encountered in populated areas throughout eastern Australia.

8 BLUE-RINGED OCTOPUS
The blue-ringed octopus is one of the most dangerous animals in the sea. The venom is produced by bacteria in the salivary glands and flows into the wound when the octopus bites. It can stop a person breathing within 10 minutes. There's no antivenom, and bites sometimes go unnoticed.

9 SYDNEY FUNNEL-WEB SPIDER
This very aggressive spider is one of the world's deadliest spiders, and a bite can kill an adult in an hour. It grows to 5 cm long and lives in burrows in the ground around the Sydney basin. With fangs that can pierce toenails, it will often strike repeatedly if disturbed.

10 REDBACK SPIDER
Females of this distinctive spider grow to 10 mm long, and are one of the most dangerous spiders in Australia. They prefer to live around houses in dry, sheltered sites among rocks, logs, junk piles, sheds and even in toilets, and are frequently disturbed by humans. Although a bite from the redback spider can be deadly, few bites are serious, and there have been no deaths since antivenom was created in 1956.

11 SCORPION
Scorpions have a fearsome reputation, but although Australia has more than 100 species, none have deadly venom. A sting from an Australian scorpion is usually no more than a painful irritation. They grow from 2 to 12 cm long and most live in remote habitats where they shelter during the day in underground burrows.

WHAT MAKES A BIRD?

BIRDS ARE THE ONLY ANIMALS with feathers, and apart from bats are the only animals capable of powered flight.

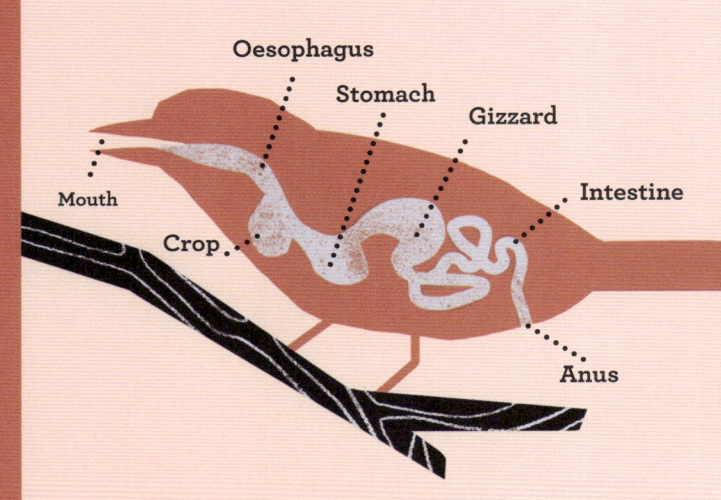

Mouth, Oesophagus, Crop, Stomach, Gizzard, Intestine, Anus

EXTRACTING ENERGY FROM FOOD

Birds need lots of energy to fly and have a special digestive system to help them break down food quickly. They have no teeth, and food goes from the mouth to the **crop** where it is stored until it moves to the **gizzard** where it is ground up with the help of small stones that the bird swallows. The crushed food is easily digested in the **intestine** to give the bird energy.

CURIOUS DISCOVERIES

This beautiful feather comes from the tail of Australia's red-tailed black cockatoo, a very large and noisy parrot of our forests and woodlands.

32

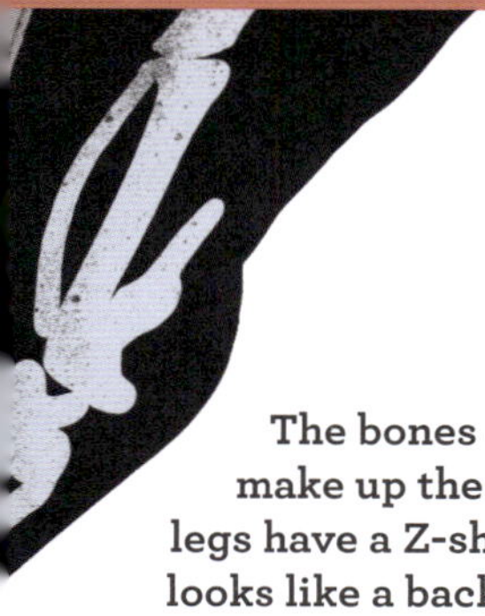

The bones of the forearms make up the wing, while their legs have a Z-shape where the ankle looks like a backward-pointing knee and the actual knee is at the top of the leg hidden among the feathers.

WINGS FIT FOR PURPOSE

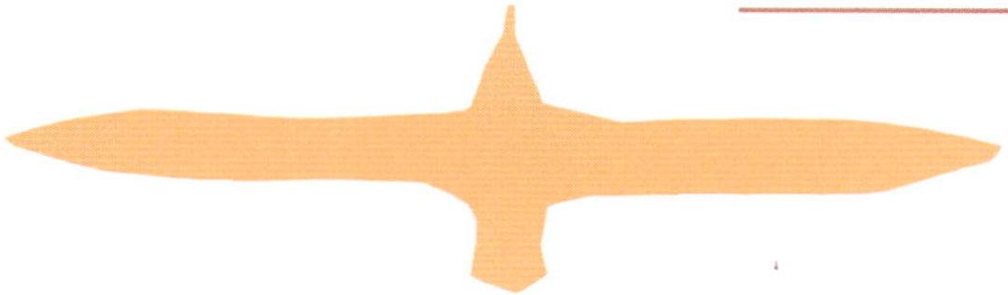

Fast flyers like swallows and falcons have long, pointed, thin wings so they can swoop and dive without using much energy.

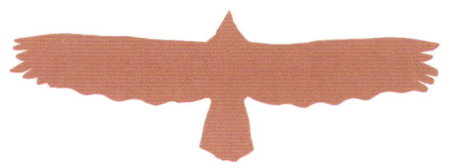

Large soaring birds like eagles and hawks have broad wings with long flight feathers to give them good control and extra lift.

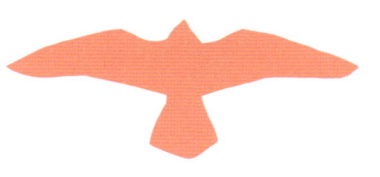

Gulls and albatrosses have long, narrow wings allowing them to glide without flapping their wings.

Highly manoeuvrable fliers like bats, robins and wrens have short, rounded wings for quick take-off and sharp turns.

LIGHTWEIGHT BONES

Flyers must keep their weight as low as possible. The bones of mammals and reptiles are solid and heavy, while those of birds are paper-thin or hollow, mostly supported inside with fine cross-struts.

WHAT BIRDS SEE

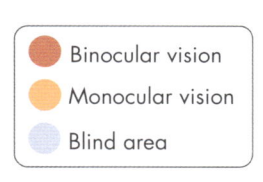

- Binocular vision
- Monocular vision
- Blind area

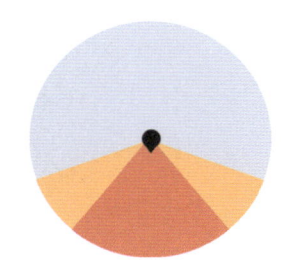

OWL

Birds of prey, like the owl, have eyes at the front of their head. They can see most of the area in front with both eyes, giving them a sharp, three-dimensional view of their prey – ideal for tracking a victim and judging its distance.

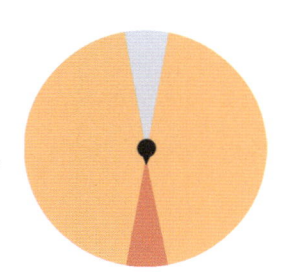

Owl visual field

PIGEON

Birds that are preyed upon, like the pigeon, have eyes at the side of their head. This gives them a better all-round view – very useful for detecting predators – but limits their three-dimensional view.

Pigeon visual field

FEATHERS

FEATHERS ARE EXTRAORDINARY. Not only do they give birds the freedom to lift off the earth, and soar and dive through the skies, but they also keep them warm in freezing places and provide coats of amazing colours.

WING
Specialised for flying, wing feathers are stiff with an interlocking structure and a narrower edge facing forwards to give them lift and prevent twisting.

CONTOUR
These are the outside feathers covering the body and streamlining its shape. They overlap like shingles and are sometimes brilliantly coloured.

FILOPLUME
These tiny hairlike feathers sense the wind speed and position of surrounding feathers to help the bird make fine adjustments during flight.

TAIL
Stiff, with an interlocking structure, tail feathers are arranged in a fan shape and control steering in flight. The tail feathers of birds such as lyrebirds have become showy ornaments.

BRISTLE
Short, stiff feathers, these are sensitive to touch and help protect the eyes.

SEMI-PLUME
Hidden beneath other feathers, semi-plume feathers are fluffy and help to keep the bird warm.

Vane

Rachis

Barb

Barb   Hooklets
       Barbule

Barb
   Barbule

DOWN
Soft and fluffy down feathers grow close to the body in between the stiff contour feathers. They trap air to keep the bird warm.

CRESTS OF BRILLIANCE
Cockatoos use their brilliant crests to communicate with other cockatoos. By raising or lowering their crests they display emotions such as excitement or alarm, warn of predators, or attempt to attract a mate.

Shaft

34

BEAKS & FEET

GRAPPLING HOOKS, PADDLES, TOOLS to grasp and shred prey, crack open nuts, sip nectar from flowers: feet and beaks have so many uses and tell us a lot about birds. Because their forelimbs have become wings, birds perform many tasks using their beaks and feet.

BEAKS

Beaks come in a variety of shapes and sizes, but even the best ones are unable to chew and break up the bird's food. This is done in a special compartment within the stomach called the **gizzard**, while the beak performs many other functions: gathering food, grooming, nest-building, feeding young and manipulating objects. In fact, you can get a very good idea about the diet and lifestyle of a bird by looking at the shape of its beak.

Prising beak: oystercatcher

Grasping beak: cormorant

Sifting beak: spoonbill

Spearing beak: heron

Probing beak: snipe

Tearing beak: falcon

Seed-cracking beak: parrot

Insect-catching beak: willy wagtail

Generalist beak: crow

FEET

Most birds have four toes, typically three facing forwards and one pointing backwards.

Some birds, like ducks and geese, cool themselves down by increasing the amount of warm blood flowing through their feet.

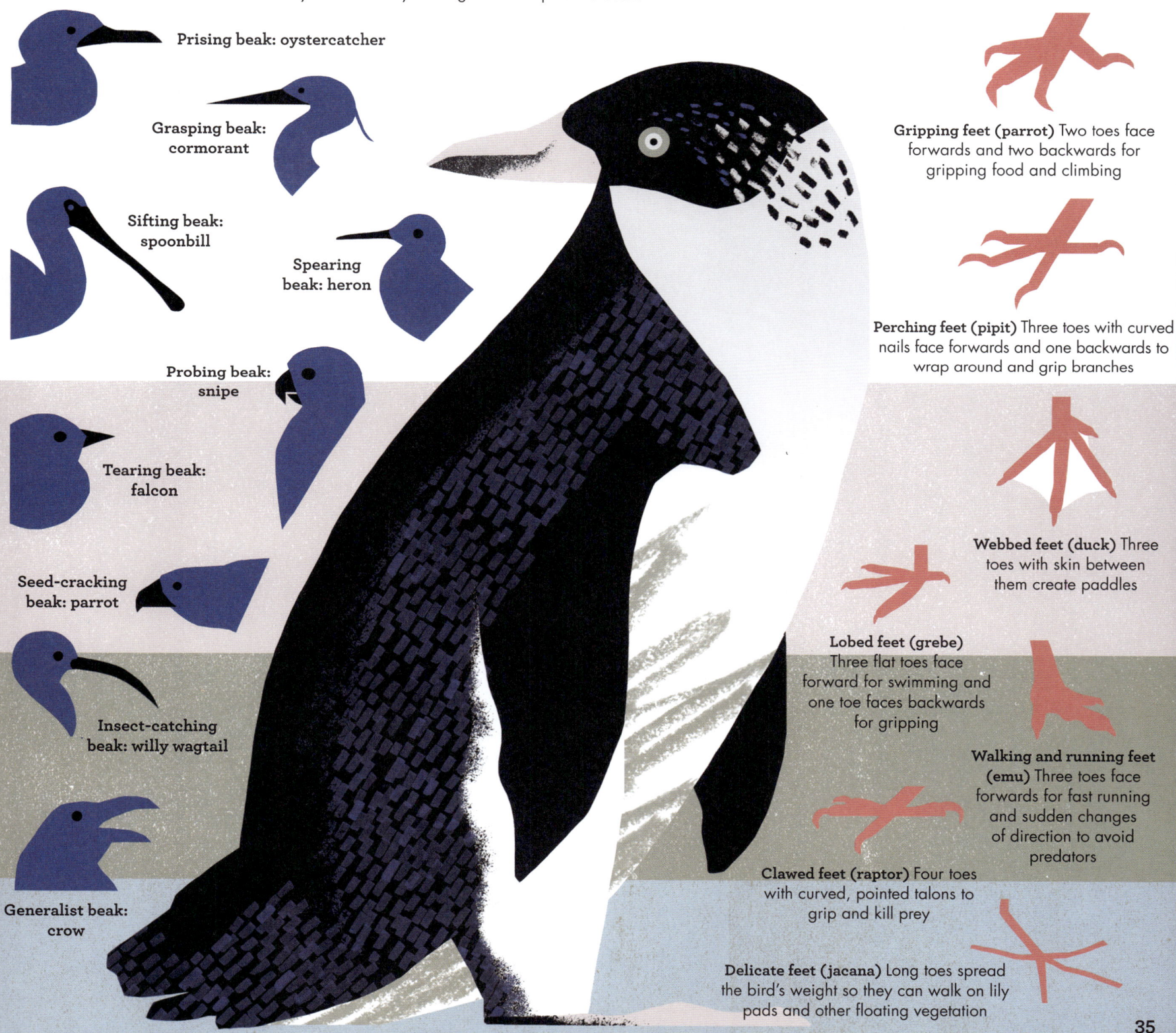

Gripping feet (parrot) Two toes face forwards and two backwards for gripping food and climbing

Perching feet (pipit) Three toes with curved nails face forwards and one backwards to wrap around and grip branches

Webbed feet (duck) Three toes with skin between them create paddles

Lobed feet (grebe) Three flat toes face forward for swimming and one toe faces backwards for gripping

Walking and running feet (emu) Three toes face forwards for fast running and sudden changes of direction to avoid predators

Clawed feet (raptor) Four toes with curved, pointed talons to grip and kill prey

Delicate feet (jacana) Long toes spread the bird's weight so they can walk on lily pads and other floating vegetation

TAKING TO THE AIR

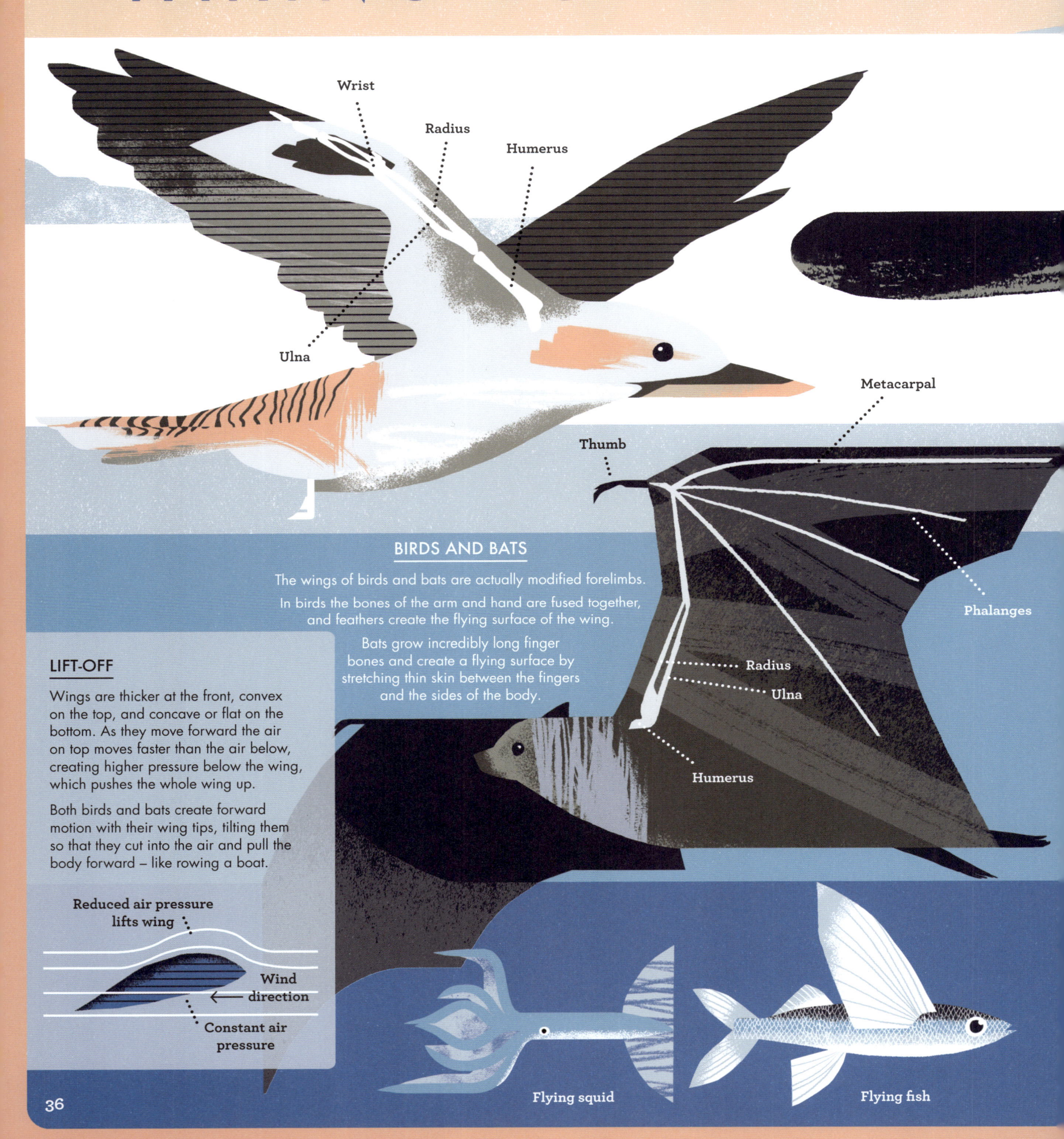

Wrist · Radius · Humerus · Ulna · Metacarpal · Thumb · Phalanges · Radius · Ulna · Humerus

BIRDS AND BATS

The wings of birds and bats are actually modified forelimbs. In birds the bones of the arm and hand are fused together, and feathers create the flying surface of the wing.

Bats grow incredibly long finger bones and create a flying surface by stretching thin skin between the fingers and the sides of the body.

LIFT-OFF

Wings are thicker at the front, convex on the top, and concave or flat on the bottom. As they move forward the air on top moves faster than the air below, creating higher pressure below the wing, which pushes the whole wing up.

Both birds and bats create forward motion with their wing tips, tilting them so that they cut into the air and pull the body forward – like rowing a boat.

Reduced air pressure lifts wing · Wind direction · Constant air pressure

Flying squid · Flying fish

36

TAKING TO THE AIR is a great way to find food and water, escape predators and travel to a warmer place to feed and breed. Fish, lizards, and even squid have managed to become airborne by using specially shaped fins or flaps of skin to glide through the air. But to stay aloft and fly more than short distances, muscles are needed to power the flapping of wings.

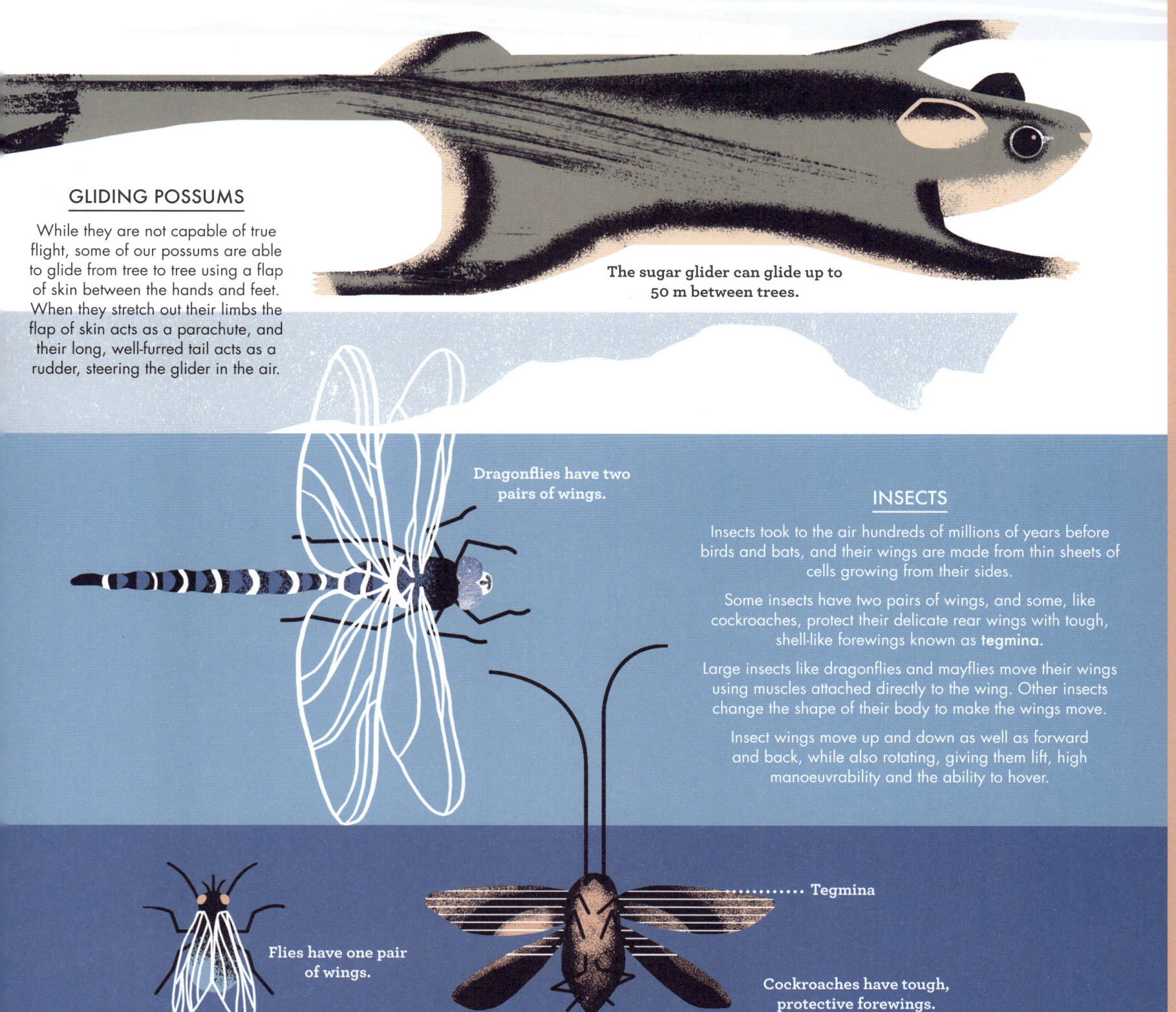

GLIDING POSSUMS

While they are not capable of true flight, some of our possums are able to glide from tree to tree using a flap of skin between the hands and feet. When they stretch out their limbs the flap of skin acts as a parachute, and their long, well-furred tail acts as a rudder, steering the glider in the air.

The sugar glider can glide up to 50 m between trees.

Dragonflies have two pairs of wings.

INSECTS

Insects took to the air hundreds of millions of years before birds and bats, and their wings are made from thin sheets of cells growing from their sides.

Some insects have two pairs of wings, and some, like cockroaches, protect their delicate rear wings with tough, shell-like forewings known as **tegmina**.

Large insects like dragonflies and mayflies move their wings using muscles attached directly to the wing. Other insects change the shape of their body to make the wings move.

Insect wings move up and down as well as forward and back, while also rotating, giving them lift, high manoeuvrability and the ability to hover.

Flies have one pair of wings.

Tegmina

Cockroaches have tough, protective forewings.

DINOSAUR BIRD

Horny casque is made from keratin, the same tough material that makes hair and nails

Brightly coloured, fleshy wattles

CASSOWARIES, WITH THEIR HELMET-LIKE casque and giant clawed feet look like toothless, beaked and feathered dinosaurs.

These huge, flightless birds have their origins in the age of the dinosaurs, between 65 and 180 million years ago, and are considered to be the dinosaurs' closest living relatives.

Like their cousin the emu, cassowaries are known as **ratites** – birds that have a flat breastbone and are unable to fly. They have small wings and hair-like glossy black feathers unsuitable for flight.

Cassowaries are dangerous. They can grow to 2 m tall and weigh 79 kg, jump up to 2 m off the ground, and won't hesitate to kick out and slash at an attacker if they feel threatened. Their feet are longer than a human hand and armed with three massive, razor-sharp claws, powerful enough to kill a human.

The cassowary's distinctive hollow helmet (**casque**) is thought to help cool the bird down by radiating heat in hot weather.

Cassowaries live in the rainforests, woodlands and mangroves of north-eastern Australia.

They are able to swallow fruit that other animals reject because it is too large or poisonous. As the cassowary moves around its large territory it helps sustain the rainforest by carrying seeds to new sites and passing them out in a pile of dung, providing a large dose of fertiliser.

Males build the nest, incubate 3–5 eggs for 50 days and raise the chicks. When they are 8–18 months old the father banishes them from his territory, leaving them to find their own patch of habitat.

Large scaly feet with dagger-like claws up to 12 cm long

Eggs weigh more than 500 g

THORNY DEVIL

ALTHOUGH IT LOOKS VERY SCARY, the thorny devil is quite harmless. No more than 20 cm long, this amazing lizard is able to live in the driest parts of Australia where there is little or no water. To escape the scorching midday heat it shelters in a shallow burrow or in the shade of low shrubs. The thorny devil's urine is thick and sludgy to make sure that it only loses the smallest amount of water. Even when it hasn't rained for months, the thorny devil is able to harvest water from the early morning dew. It does this by covering itself in damp sand. Water soaks into microscopic channels that cover its scaly skin and travels to the corners of its mouth.

The thorny devil eats only ants, by the thousands, flicking them into its mouth with its tongue.

Females lay soft-shelled eggs in a burrow dug into the sand. When they hatch, the tiny newborn thorny devils eat their egg cases, and this gives them enough energy to dig their way out of the burrow.

Fat is stored in the tail and keeps the lizard alive when it hibernates over winter.

If threatened the lizard drops its head between its front legs, confronting the attacker with a fat-filled double-spined hump.

Sharp spines discourage predators.

Scaly skin reduces water loss.

Sandy colours and irregular shapes help it blend in with the surroundings.

Droplets of water from damp sand and morning dew flow in tiny channels between the scales to the corners of the lizard's mouth.

RADICAL REPTILES

REPTILES HAVE BEEN ON the planet for more than 300 million years – far longer than the mammals and birds – and Australia is home to 917 of the world's 8734 different reptile species. Among Australia's reptiles are endearing turtles and tiny skinks; the estuarine crocodile, the largest and most fearsome predator on earth; and the mainland taipan, the world's deadliest snake.

Reptiles have one great advantage over the birds and mammals: they need far less food to survive. Instead of using most of their food to keep warm, reptiles (along with frogs, fish, insects and many other animals) get all the heat they need from their surroundings. These animals are known as cold-blooded or **ectothermic**. When it is cool, they are sluggish and warm themselves up in the sun. When it is too hot, they retreat to the shade. In very cold conditions their body processes slow down and they go into a sleep-like state known as torpor, only waking up when the temperature rises.

Ectothermic animals have one major disadvantage: they cannot survive in very cold places like the Antarctic. Most Australian reptiles live in the deserts and warmer parts of the continent.

All reptiles have tough, scaly skin that must be shed to allow them to grow. Their skin is also waterproof (which helps them conserve water), and in the case of the crocodiles and turtles forms a tough body armour.

Although a few reptiles give birth to live young, most lay leathery-shelled eggs in a burrow or crevice where they are left to hatch on their own. Without any help from their parents, not many survive to become adults.

Some reptiles spend part or all of their lives in trees, and many geckos have enlarged toes with hundreds of tiny overlapping plates on the soles. These act like suction pads and allow the gecko to grip smooth surfaces, climb vertically and run upside down.

LIZARDS

There are more types of lizards than any other reptiles in Australia, and they come in many forms. Most have four powerful legs, a long tail and a small head. A few lizards have no legs at all and are easily mistaken for snakes. Their bodies are covered in scales of an amazing variety of colours and shapes. Some lizards have frills, horns and brightly coloured spots or tongues. When attacked, many are able to detach part or all of their tail, leaving it wriggling on the ground to distract a predator, giving them a chance to escape. A new tail grows to replace the lost one.

TURTLES

Turtles carry a tough shell to protect them from predators. They live in the sea and on land, and some travel long distances to find waterholes or a place to nest. In droughts they bury themselves in the mud and await the rain. Some Australian sea turtles grow to 1.5 m long and can live for more than 60 years.

CROCODILES

Crocodiles are Australia's fiercest predators, with thick horny skin covering bony body armour. They lie in wait close to the water's edge with only their eyes and nostrils above water, ready to ambush any creature that comes within range. Female crocodiles are among the few reptiles to look after their young, guarding their eggs and often carrying hatchlings to the water in their mouths.

SNAKES

Snakes have no limbs, eyelids or external ears, but they can swim, climb trees and travel at up to 10 kph on land. Snakes are stealthy hunters. They kill by injecting powerful venom into animals through hollow teeth called fangs, or by squeezing their prey in the coils of their muscular body until the animal suffocates. With elastic skin and jaws that come apart, snakes can swallow animals much larger than their own heads. It takes a long time to digest a large animal, and snakes can go for months without eating.

CURIOUS DISCOVERIES

Snakes leave their old skins behind as they grow. This long, parchment-like snakeskin belonged to Australia's largest snake – the scrub python. Growing to 8.5 m long, a scrub python can devour a whole kangaroo in one go. Pythons big and small are often found in the roof spaces of Australian houses. Luckily for us, they aren't poisonous or aggressive, but they do have lots of small teeth to grab their prey, and will happily consume mice, cats, possums and even small dogs.

MASTERS OF DISGUISE

NATURE HAS DEVISED SURPRISING and ingenious ways to evade predators and sneak up on prey. Many creatures rely on camouflage to disappear into the background while others are able to change their identity to make them look more dangerous to predators to avoid being eaten, or less dangerous to avoid intimidating their prey.

Some animals hide in plain sight by masquerading as something that is bad to eat or dangerous. This is known as **mimesis** and is very common among insects.

① TAWNY FROGMOUTH
When perched on a tree the colours and streaked patterns of the tawny frogmouth's feathers blend in with the bark and branches.

② LEAFY SEA DRAGON
With delicate, leaf-shaped structures all over its body, the leafy sea dragon blends perfectly into its seaweed habitat.

③ GIANT CUTTLEFISH
Australia's friendly and curious giant cuttlefish is one of the world's greatest mimics. When it wants to disappear it changes the colours and patterns of its skin in an instant to perfectly match the background. It can also alter its body shape to look exactly like a piece of seaweed, rock, sand or even another marine creature.

④ NORTHERN LEAF-TAILED GECKO
This tree-dwelling gecko of Australia's northern rainforests flattens itself against the bark with its head facing down. The gecko's broken outlines and lichen-like patterns make it almost invisible in its rainforest home.

CURIOUS DISCOVERIES

Often found washed up on Australian beaches, this smooth, white, lightweight object is the internal shell of a cuttlefish. By pumping air in and out of this spongy material, the cuttlefish controls its buoyancy, allowing it to rise or sink in the water.

⑤ LEAF KATYDID
Leaf katydids are found all over Australia. They look so much like a leaf, even with detailed veins, that they are almost impossible to detect against a leafy background.

⑥ MEADOW ARGUS
The eyespots on the wings of the meadow argus butterfly look like those of a much larger animal and deter predators who think they are facing a dangerous creature. Many butterflies and moths have hidden eyespots which they flash at attackers to frighten them off.

⑦ PINK UNDERWING MOTH CATERPILLAR
The caterpillar of the pink underwing moth looks like a dried leaf, but when threatened it rears up with its real head curled under its body, revealing a large false head complete with bright eyespots and markings that look like teeth.

43

METAMORPHOSIS

CATERPILLARS CHANGING INTO beautiful butterflies, legless tadpoles becoming hopping frogs – extraordinary transformations happen in the lives of insects, amphibians and crustaceans. These changes are known as metamorphosis, which is Greek for 'a transforming'.

CURIOUS DISCOVERIES

This large silk cocoon has been created by the caterpillar of the Hercules moth. Inside the cocoon the caterpillar's body is dissolving into a soup and being remade into a completely different animal: a winged creature that will mate and lay eggs. Such dramatic life-changes allow these animals to live in completely different habitats and eat different food as they metamorphose from one form to another. This gives them a much better chance of survival in an ever-changing world.

HERCULES MOTH

Living in the tropical rainforests of Australia, with a wingspan of up to 30 cm, this is the world's largest moth. The moth's spectacular yellow-spiked, bluish-green caterpillar is an eating machine, munching through leaves at an astonishing rate, growing to 12 cm before metamorphosing into a huge flying adult.

Surprisingly, the adults have no mouth parts and are therefore unable to feed. Instead of wasting time looking for food, their short lives are dedicated to looking for a mate to breed with and produce the next generation. It can be hard to find each other in the rainforest, so the females produce a powerful scent that males can smell up to 2 km away.

INCOMPLETE METAMORPHOSIS

Some insects such as grasshoppers, cicadas, cockroaches and dragonflies develop from an egg directly into a smaller form of the adult, known as a **nymph**.

- The nymph gradually increases in size by moulting (shedding its old skin).
- After each moult, the nymph looks slightly different until it finally develops into the adult form.
- This is called **incomplete metamorphosis**.

Egg → Nymph → Adult

44

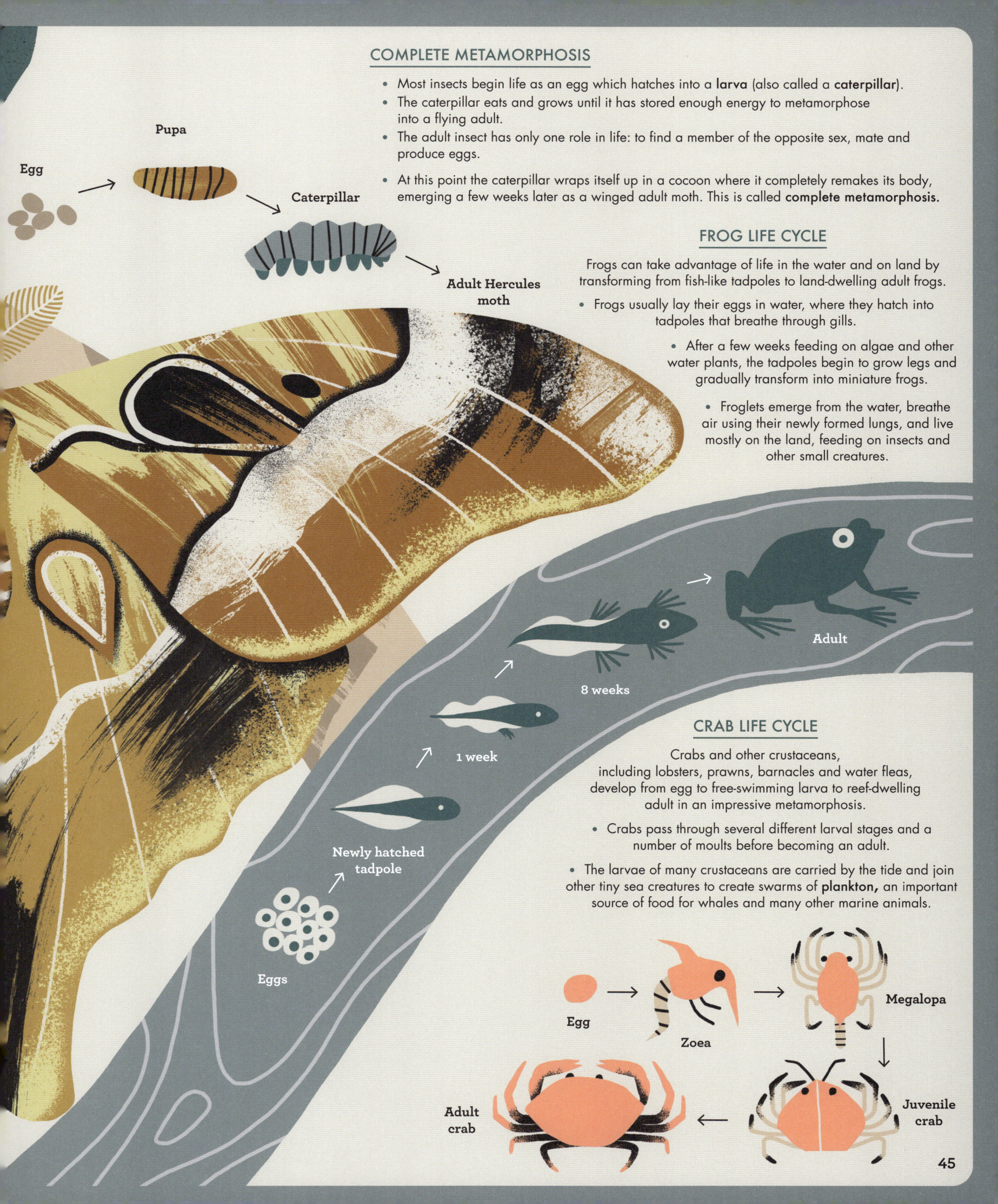

COMPLETE METAMORPHOSIS

- Most insects begin life as an egg which hatches into a **larva** (also called a **caterpillar**).
- The caterpillar eats and grows until it has stored enough energy to metamorphose into a flying adult.
- The adult insect has only one role in life: to find a member of the opposite sex, mate and produce eggs.
- At this point the caterpillar wraps itself up in a cocoon where it completely remakes its body, emerging a few weeks later as a winged adult moth. This is called **complete metamorphosis**.

Egg → Pupa → Caterpillar → Adult Hercules moth

FROG LIFE CYCLE

Frogs can take advantage of life in the water and on land by transforming from fish-like tadpoles to land-dwelling adult frogs.

- Frogs usually lay their eggs in water, where they hatch into tadpoles that breathe through gills.
- After a few weeks feeding on algae and other water plants, the tadpoles begin to grow legs and gradually transform into miniature frogs.
- Froglets emerge from the water, breathe air using their newly formed lungs, and live mostly on the land, feeding on insects and other small creatures.

Eggs → Newly hatched tadpole → 1 week → 8 weeks → Adult

CRAB LIFE CYCLE

Crabs and other crustaceans, including lobsters, prawns, barnacles and water fleas, develop from egg to free-swimming larva to reef-dwelling adult in an impressive metamorphosis.

- Crabs pass through several different larval stages and a number of moults before becoming an adult.
- The larvae of many crustaceans are carried by the tide and join other tiny sea creatures to create swarms of **plankton,** an important source of food for whales and many other marine animals.

Egg → Zoea → Megalopa → Juvenile crab → Adult crab

FABULOUS FROGS

FROGS AND TOADS, SALAMANDERS, newts and worm-like caecilians are all **amphibians** – cold-blooded vertebrates adapted to live both in and out of water. They evolved from fleshy-finned fish more than 300 million years ago, but frogs are the only amphibians native to Australia.

It may seem strange that the driest habitable continent has the most varied range of frogs in the world – Australia has more than 240 species. They live in our rainforests, wetlands, mountains and deserts, and many have adapted their ways of living to cope with extended droughts and short wet seasons. An occasional inflow of water, either from the sky or from temporary waterways, is usually sufficient to support a frog population.

All frogs are carnivores, eating virtually any small animal that will fit into their mouth. Most are, however, incapable of swallowing anything larger than insects, other arthropods and earthworms. Larger frogs occasionally eat small reptiles and other frogs. Prey is detected by sight and is typically caught with the frog's long, muscular, sticky tongue.

Frogs absorb water through the skin on their undersides and never need to drink. Most can change colour within a few hours or days to absorb or reflect heat or to match their surroundings and avoid being seen by predators.

- Bulging eyes to see nearly all directions
- Eardrum – frogs have an amazing sense of hearing
- Can change colour
- Semi-permeable skin – frogs can absorb water and breathe through their skin
- Feet adapted for swimming, climbing or digging
- Powerful hind legs

FROG FEET

- Webbed feet for swimming
- Sticky pads and wide-spaced toes for climbing
- Powerful, stubby toes with a horny pad for digging

FROGS IN TREES

Most frogs prefer warm, moist habitats, and in the coastal forests many species have taken to the trees. Tree frogs have grooved discs or pads on the tips of their fingers and toes that allow them to 'stick' onto leaves and other smooth, vertical surfaces. In the dry season they hide in the moist bases of leaves to prevent dehydration.

FROGS IN THE DESERT

Burrowing deep underground to avoid heat and drought, water-holding frogs pop up after rain to breed and eat. Short arms and legs and a big round body help them store and conserve water, and in their underground chamber these frogs create an amazing waxy cocoon that forms a waterproof skin around them. With only their nostrils exposed, they can remain underground for years without drying out.

POISONOUS FROGS

Some frogs, like the crucifix frog, can secrete poisonous fluids from glands in their skin. To deter predators, this frog has a distinctive reddish cross on its back.

Vocal sac

Frogs are more likely to be heard than seen, and their distinctive calls are a useful aid to identification. Most are nocturnal, and the chorus of thousands of calling males can be deafening on moist summer evenings. To amplify their call, frogs puff out a **vocal sac** in front of their throat.

Dung beetle

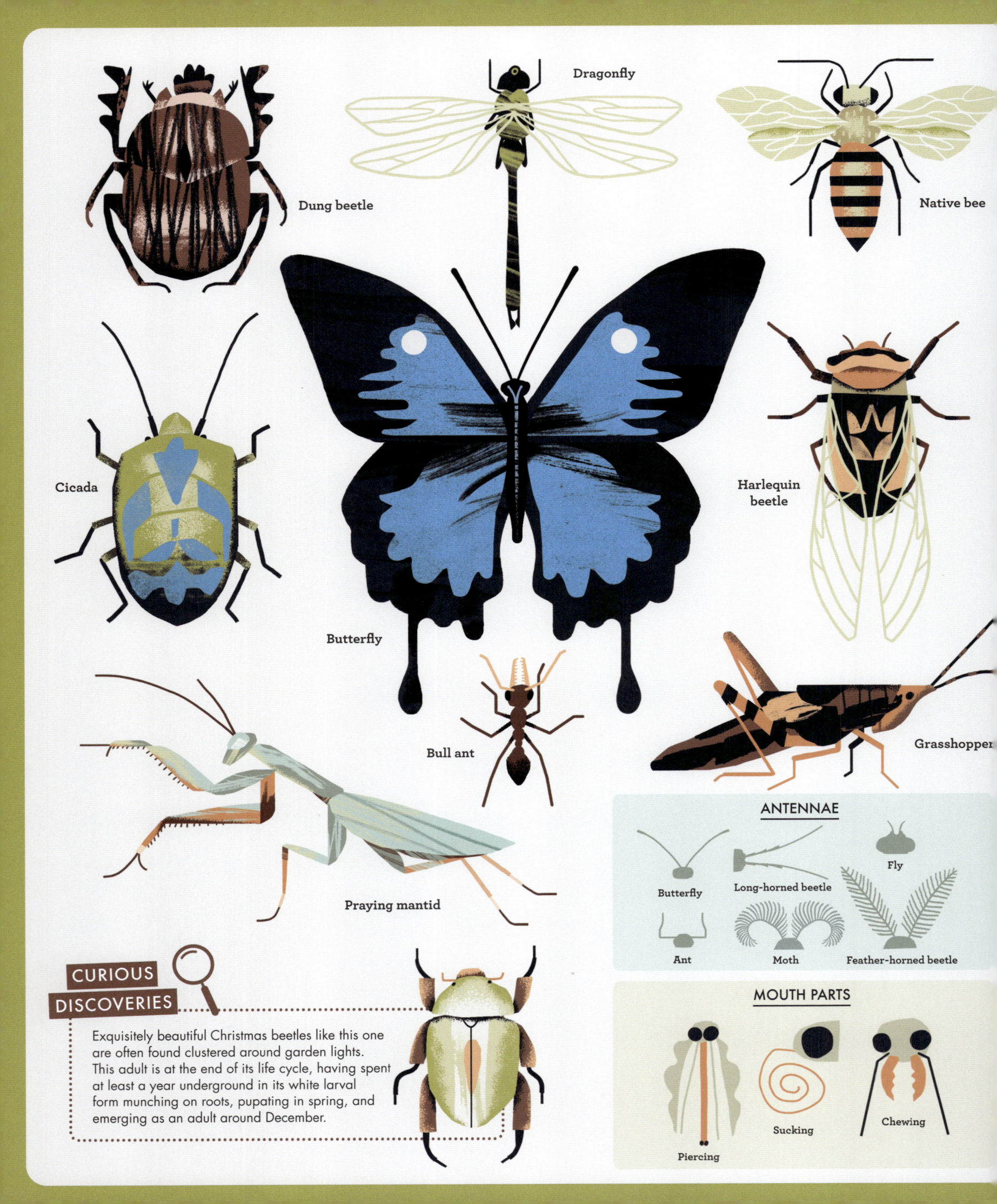

Dragonfly

Native bee

Cicada

Butterfly

Harlequin beetle

Bull ant

Grasshopper

Praying mantid

ANTENNAE

Butterfly

Long-horned beetle

Fly

Ant

Moth

Feather-horned beetle

MOUTH PARTS

Piercing

Sucking

Chewing

CURIOUS DISCOVERIES

Exquisitely beautiful Christmas beetles like this one are often found clustered around garden lights. This adult is at the end of its life cycle, having spent at least a year underground in its white larval form munching on roots, pupating in spring, and emerging as an adult around December.

INCREDIBLE INSECTS

INSECTS ARE THE MOST SUCCESSFUL creatures on earth. No other animals can match them for their diversity and abundance. Their numbers are so vast that for each human alive today there are more than a million insects. Insects make up over 90 per cent of all animals, and there are at least 200,000 insect species living in Australia, with up to 30 million species in the world. Most are still awaiting discovery, and there is a pretty good chance some of the insects you come across have not yet been officially identified.

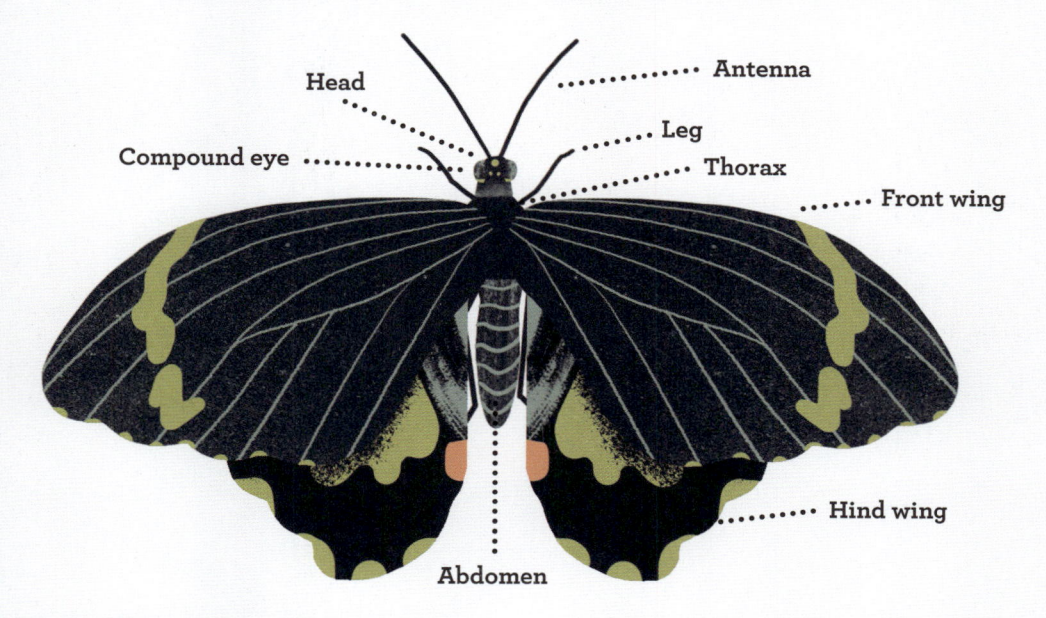

Labels: Head, Antenna, Compound eye, Leg, Thorax, Front wing, Hind wing, Abdomen

WHAT MAKES AN INSECT?

- Insects, along with crabs, crayfish, scorpions, spiders, millipedes and centipedes, are **arthropods**, which in Greek means 'jointed foot'. All arthropods have a tough outer skeleton, resembling armour. Their body is divided into segments, with pairs of jointed limbs.
- Insects have a body divided into three segments – the head, thorax and abdomen.
- Most insects have large **compound eyes** made up of hundreds of tiny units with their own lens, known as **ommatidia**.
- All insects have highly sensitive antennae that detect touch, taste and smell.
- Insects can swim, fly, crawl and burrow, and live almost everywhere, from steaming hot volcanic springs to the ice caps of the poles.
- Many insects have wings, giving them the opportunity to travel long distances to find food, safety and mates.
- Insects do not have lungs. Air enters their body through holes in the exoskeleton called **spiracles**. These connect to a network of tubes that delivers oxygen-rich air to cells in the body and carries away carbon dioxide.
- Without insects, most flowering plants would not be pollinated.
- Insects are a source of food for many creatures.
- Insects help to clean up the environment by consuming dead plants and animals.
- Insects develop by **metamorphosis,** beginning life as an egg that either hatches into a larval form completely different to the adult, or as a miniature version of the adult, called a **nymph**. Insect larvae (caterpillars) pupate before emerging as an adult, whereas nymphs shed their skins (**moult**) as they grow into full-sized adults.

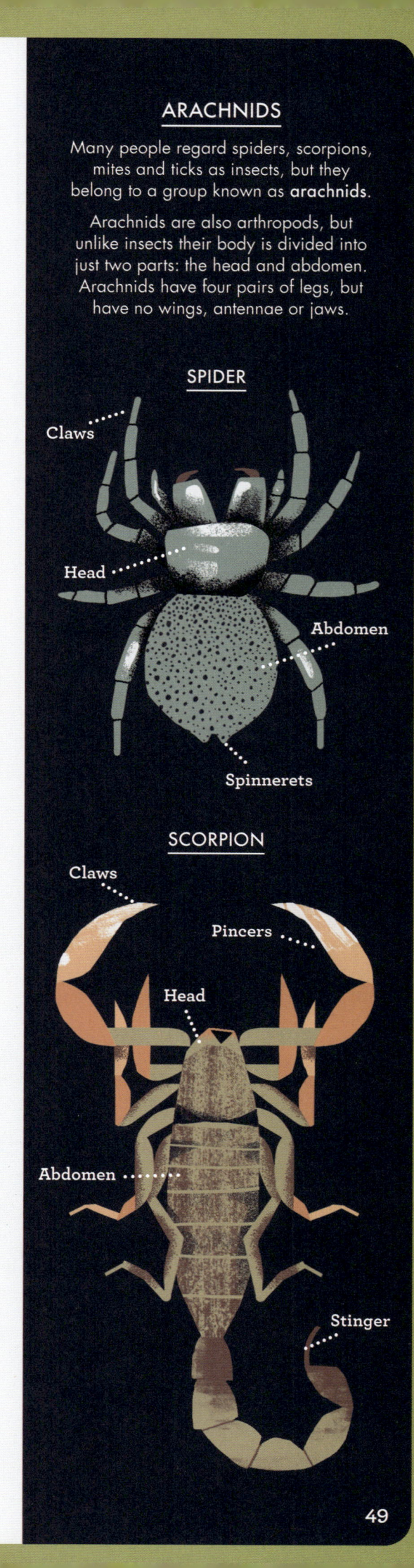

ARACHNIDS

Many people regard spiders, scorpions, mites and ticks as insects, but they belong to a group known as **arachnids**.

Arachnids are also arthropods, but unlike insects their body is divided into just two parts: the head and abdomen. Arachnids have four pairs of legs, but have no wings, antennae or jaws.

SPIDER

Labels: Claws, Head, Abdomen, Spinnerets

SCORPION

Labels: Claws, Pincers, Head, Abdomen, Stinger

DAZZLING DISPLAYS

FROM INTRICATE DANCES TO beautiful pageants of colour, many Australian animals have developed dazzling visual displays to attract mates, scare off aggressors or warn intruders to stay away.

BLUE-RINGED OCTOPUS
A bite from this small and colourful octopus can kill an adult human in minutes. Rather than use its venom, the octopus warns attackers to stay away by changing its body colours and patterns in the blink of an eye, creating bright iridescent blue rings flashing against a yellow background.

CURIOUS DISCOVERIES

Found on a sandbar next to a forest of mangroves lining a tidal estuary, this distinctive claw belongs to the two-toned fiddler crab.

This is no ordinary crab. The males have one enormous, colourful claw that they wave around to attract the attention of female fiddler crabs.

PEACOCK SPIDER
Only about 5 mm long, male peacock spiders perform a dazzling courtship dance, waving their black-and-white tipped legs and flipping up two brilliantly coloured peacock-like flaps from their abdomen.

FRILLED LIZARD
To scare away other lizards or predators, this dragon lizard rears up on its hind legs, gapes widely showing its bright yellow mouth, and erects the frill of coloured skin around its neck.

MAGNIFICENT RIFLEBIRD
Showing off his brilliant blue-green breast, a male magnificent riflebird performs his courtship dance: hopping up and down a branch, swinging his head from side to side while fanning his wings and tail feathers.

FIDDLER CRAB
Fiddler crabs live with thousands of others, each with their own burrow. When a female is ready to mate, she wanders through the colony and all the males wave their large claws to attract her attention. She chooses her preferred male and follows him into his burrow to mate.

51

ANIMAL ARCHITECTS

ANIMALS ARE AMAZING ARCHITECTS, creating mounds, burrows, nests and shells. They design their home as a place to store food, attract a mate or raise their young, much like human structures.

SATIN BOWERBIRD
The iridescent blue male satin bowerbird builds an elaborate structure decorated with sticks and carefully arranged brightly coloured objects. His purpose is to entice a female to his artistic bower and convince her that he has the skills to be the best partner to raise their offspring.

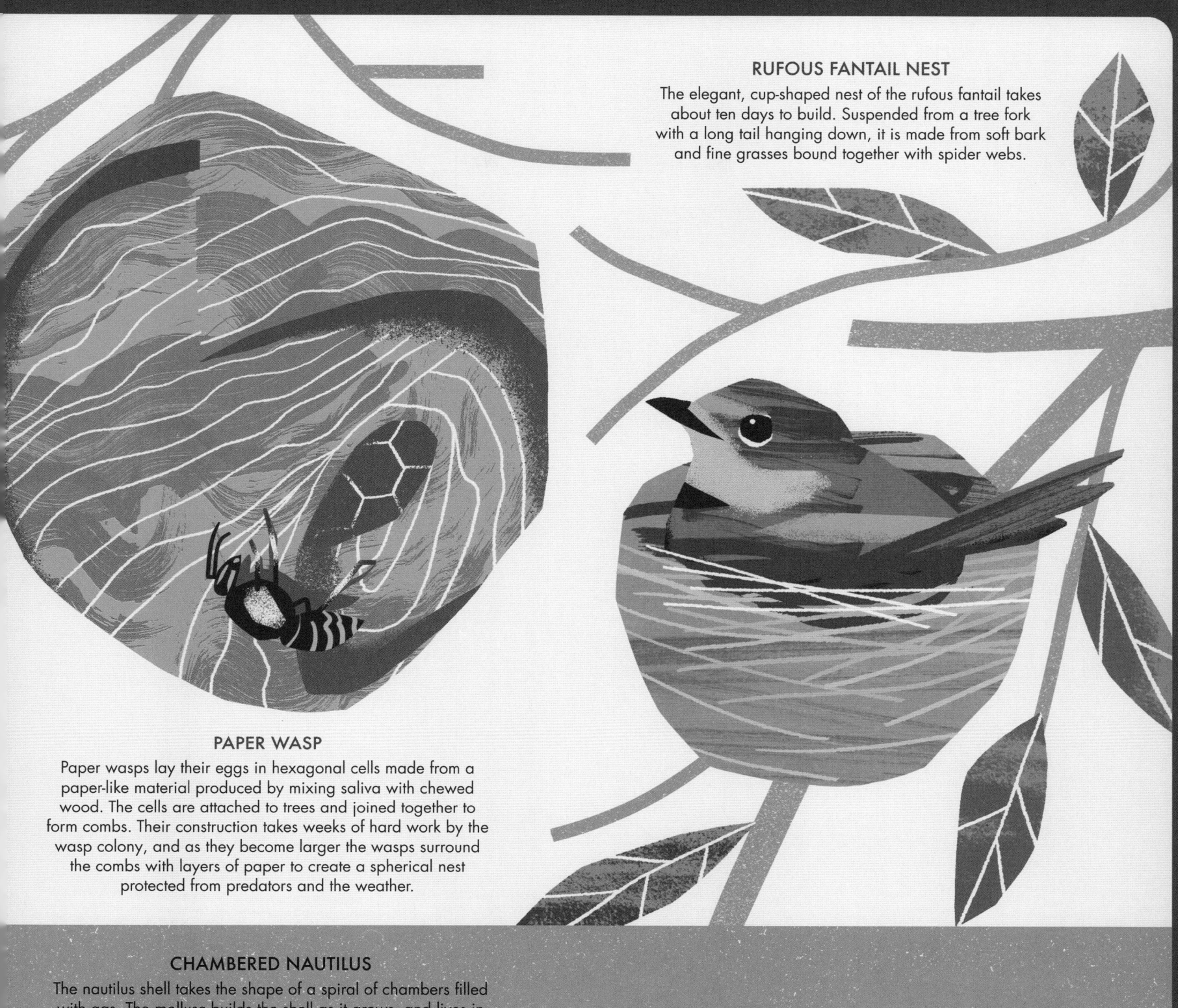

RUFOUS FANTAIL NEST
The elegant, cup-shaped nest of the rufous fantail takes about ten days to build. Suspended from a tree fork with a long tail hanging down, it is made from soft bark and fine grasses bound together with spider webs.

PAPER WASP
Paper wasps lay their eggs in hexagonal cells made from a paper-like material produced by mixing saliva with chewed wood. The cells are attached to trees and joined together to form combs. Their construction takes weeks of hard work by the wasp colony, and as they become larger the wasps surround the combs with layers of paper to create a spherical nest protected from predators and the weather.

CHAMBERED NAUTILUS
The nautilus shell takes the shape of a spiral of chambers filled with gas. The mollusc builds the shell as it grows, and lives in the outermost chamber of the spiral. By pumping water in or out of the chambers, the nautilus adjusts its buoyancy so that it can float up towards the surface or sink to the depths of the ocean.

CURIOUS DISCOVERIES
This exquisitely crafted shell has been created by a marine mollusc — the **nautilus** — to protect its soft body parts. It is just one example of the patience, skill and cooperation that many animals use to design and build beautiful and complex structures to help them survive.

CATHEDRALS OF CLAY

Hooded parrot

THESE IMPOSING, CATHEDRAL-LIKE MOUNDS of clay are created by insects no more than 5 mm long, and are among the tallest non-human-made structures in the world. Built by spinifex termites, they can rise 8 m above the ground, and house as many as three million termites.

Found in the savanna grasslands of tropical northern Australia, cathedral termite mounds are constructed over many years by armies of blind worker termites who mix together tiny balls of saliva, plant matter, soil and faeces, and somehow manage to place each ball in exactly the right position to build this remarkable structure.

- An intricate system of passages permeates the mound, as well as food storage and nursery chambers, and a royal chamber at the centre to house the queen.

- The queen's sole purpose is to lay eggs. She can lay 3000 eggs each day, and is cared for by a small army of young termite nymphs who clean and feed her and carry the eggs to the nursery chambers.

- The tough outer layer and network of passages provide year-round protection from the sun, wind, rain and bushfires, and control the warmth, moisture and ventilation inside the mound.

- Long underground tunnels head out from the mound to grassy areas, and workers travel back and forth, returning with chewed grass stalks to feed the colony. Termites are, in fact, some of nature's most important recycling agents.

- Soldier termites, known as **nasutes**, defend the colony from invading ants and other predators by coating them in a transparent sticky substance squirted through their long, tubular snout.

- Birds and other animals shelter in cracks and crevices in the mound, including the beautiful but rare hooded parrot, which nests in holes chewed into the mound.

Royal chamber

Underground tunnels

Termites

POND LIFE

Damselfly

Mallard duck

Azure kingfisher

Dragonfly

Long-necked turtle

Frog

Water strider

Rainbowfish

Gudgeon

Tadpole

Yabby

Pond snail

Freshwater mussel

Mosquito larvae

Diving beetle

WATER IS ESSENTIAL TO LIFE, and if you take a close look at a pond you will find a world teeming with life. Frogs, birds, turtles and hordes of water-loving insects find food, shelter and places to breed here, while below the surface is a world of tadpoles, mosquito larvae, fish, molluscs, crustaceans, beetles and an abundance of tiny creatures, many too small to see without a microscope.

Sunlight reaching the bottom of a pond encourages plants to grow, providing food for fish, crustaceans and insects. The larvae of mosquitoes and the tadpoles of frogs feed and mature below the surface while birds, amphibians and turtles dip in and out of the water looking for food.

55

GREAT BAR

EXTENDING FOR 2300 KM along the north-eastern coast of Australia, the Great Barrier Reef is the largest structure in the world made by living organisms, and home to a greater number of fish species than anywhere on earth.

CURIOUS DISCOVERIES

Like the branches of a leafless tree, this piece of red coral was created by tiny organisms called **coral polyps** beneath the warm, shallow waters of Australia's Great Barrier Reef.

RIER REEF

Zooxanthellae colour the coral

Tentacles armed with stinging cells to capture prey

Mouth

Stomach

Limestone skeleton

CORAL POLYPS: ARCHITECTS OF THE REEF

Coral polyps are an extraordinary group of animals that appear to be more like rocks than living creatures. Coral polyps often live together in large colonies in warm, shallow water. They snatch tiny floating animals from the water with their stinging tentacles and build hard cases or tubes to protect themselves.

Over hundreds or thousands of years these cases build up to create massive coral reefs, providing homes to myriad sea creatures.

Most coral polyps have clear bodies, and their amazing colours come from the millions of microscopic algae – called **zooxanthellae** – living inside their tentacles. The algae produce different coloured pigments that show through the polyp's clear body, giving coral its beautiful colour.

The coral provides a home for the algae, which in turn help to nourish the coral polyps. But when the coral is stressed by heat or pollution, the polyps eject the algae and turn white. If conditions return to normal the polyps can regain the algae and their colour.

REEF DWELLERS

THE WARM, SHALLOW WATERS of the Great Barrier Reef, together with the network of canyons and caverns created by billions of coral polyps, provide food, shelter, hunting grounds and hiding places for an incredible number of fish and other fascinating marine creatures.

1 BISCUIT SEA STAR	5 CLOWNFISH	9 HAIRY SEA URCHIN	13 SEAHORSE
2 BLUE-RINGED OCTOPUS	6 CRUSTACEAN	10 LEOPARD SEA CUCUMBER	14 SEA SNAKE
3 BOX JELLYFISH	7 DUGONG	11 LIONFISH	15 SEA SLUG
4 CHRISTMAS TREE WORM	8 MANTA RAY	12 REEF SHARK	16 TURTLE

BLUE-RINGED OCTOPUS

THE BLUE-RINGED OCTOPUS has blue blood, three hearts, nine brains and enough venom to kill 26 humans.

Chromatophore cells
Small pigment cells in the skin vary in colour. By expanding some and contracting others the octopus changes colour in response to its mood or surroundings.

Large central brain
With one large central brain and a smaller brain in each arm, octopuses are the most intelligent of the invertebrates, rivalling many mammals.

Mantle
This is the body of the octopus.

Two large eyes
It has excellent eyesight.

Eight arms
These muscular arms are used to move around and capture prey. An octopus can regenerate an injured or lost arm in about six weeks.

Siphon
Water squirted from this tube pushes the octopus along.

Suckers
Each arm has two rows of suckers. They can move independently and are sensitive to taste and touch.

- This small, beautiful, yet deadly cephalopod lives in rock pools all around the coast of Australia.
- Although it will fit in the palm of an adult's hand, its venomous bite can kill a person in less than 30 minutes.
- It has a parrot-like beak underneath the body used to cut into shells, and to bite and paralyse fish, crustaceans and other marine animals with nerve poison.
- It hides in crevices and shells, emerging to feed or mate, crawling along using its eight long arms, or propelling itself with water squirted from a tube at the base of the arms.
- It changes colour according to its mood or surroundings, but when threatened its blue markings become vividly iridescent. As well as changing colour, it can change its body shape to imitate its surroundings and squeeze into rocky crevices where it hides.
- It has excellent vision and the suckers on its arms are sensitive to taste and touch.
- The female lays only one clutch of 60–100 eggs in her lifetime and carries them under her arms until they hatch about 50 days later. She does not eat during this time and dies soon after they hatch.

MARVELLOUS MARINE INVERTEBRATES

DAZZLING CORALS, SPONGES, JELLYFISH, squid and octopuses, starfish, crabs and fascinating marine worms – all are marine invertebrates. This vast and varied group of animals without backbones includes some of the most beautiful and extraordinary creatures on earth, and to find them all you need to do is explore Australia's beaches, rockpools and coastal waterways. Some are too small to see with just your eyes, while others, like the giant squid, can grow to more than 13 m.

CNIDARIANS

Corals, jellyfish and sea anemones belong to a group of animals with stinging cells known as **cnidocytes.** These cells contain coiled, barbed threads, often loaded with poison, and are fired when touched by passing prey. All have a hollow, bell-shaped body with one opening (the mouth) fringed with tentacles armed with cnidocytes. They have no brain or organs like heart and lungs.

4 JELLYFISH
These free-swimming cnidarians move by expanding and contracting their umbrella-shaped bell to create a jet of water that pushes them along. Tentacles dotted with cnidocytes trail below to paralyse and capture passing fish.

5 CORAL
Coral reefs are made from millions of tiny soft-bodied cnidarians (coral polyps) with a hard, protective limestone base called a calicle.

6 SEA ANEMONE
Sea anemones spend most of their time attached by their adhesive foot to rocks or the sea floor, waiting for fish to come close enough to be trapped by their colourful stinging tentacles.

The clownfish and sea anemone live together in a relationship that benefits both parties (called a **symbiotic** relationship). The anemone protects the fish with its stinging tentacles and feeds on scraps from the clownfish's meals. Clownfish have a layer of slime covering their skin that protects them from the anemone's tentacles.

4 Jellyfish
5 Coral
6 Sea anemone
6 Clownfish

ECHINODERMS

8 This group includes starfish, sea urchins and sea cucumbers. All have a shell-like skeleton (**exoskeleton**) covered by skin, often with spiny projections. A network of water-filled tubes carries food and gases around the body and helps the animal move by pumping water through hundreds of tiny tube-like feet that poke through their exoskeleton. Groups of feet move together to create a wave that pushes the animal along.

CRUSTACEANS

9 Crabs, lobsters, shrimp, barnacles and krill all belong to this group. They have joined legs and are protected by a tough exoskeleton. They sense the outside world through two compound eyes (usually on stalks) and two pairs of antennae.

9 Lobster

8 Sea urchin

8 Starfish

9 Crab

3 Bivalve sea snail

1 Nautilus

2 Sea slug

3 Cone shell

MOLLUSCS

Molluscs are soft-bodied animals covered by an outer layer called a **mantle**. Some molluscs protect themselves with a tough outer shell, while others have developed some amazing ways to defend themselves.

1 **CEPHALOPODS**

This group of molluscs includes the octopus, squid, cuttlefish and nautilus. Some release a cloud of black ink into the water to confuse a predator and cover their escape. Many also have a beak-like mouth with a venomous bite and suckers on their arms or tentacles to help them catch and hold their prey.

2 **NUDIBRANCHS**

Also known as sea slugs, they are among the most flamboyant of all sea life. Vivid colours and patterns warn predators that they may be poisonous. Some nudibranchs are armed with stinging cells (**cnidocytes**) stolen from the jellyfish and anemones they eat.

3 **SEA SNAILS**

Most sea snails protect their soft bodies with a hard outer shell, usually spiralling to a point. Some have a hinged shell that snaps shut to keep the animal safe inside. Most are herbivores, some, like the cone snails, capture and paralyse small creatures using tiny barbed darts tipped with a powerful venom.

61

Sugar glider

Cicada

Wedge-tailed eagle

Goanna

Powerful owl

Tree frog

Kingfisher

62

TREE LIFE

TREES ARE FULL OF LIFE, and the older they become the more life they support. Some trees live for hundreds of years. Over its long life this old eucalypt has developed many hollows, cracks and crevices. Termites have eaten out the soft heartwood, leaving places for animals large and small to live, breed and shelter.

- Eucalypt flowers are the forest's richest source of nectar, and many trees only produce nectar at night to attract flying foxes and other hungry nocturnal nectar-loving animals.
- Birds of prey build their nests in the highest branches where they can watch for prey.
- Dead leaves and litter enrich the soil and provide habitat for microorganisms, snails, insects, arachnids, frogs and lizards.
- Hollow trunks and limbs are sheltering and breeding sites for birds, bats, possums and gliders.
- Tree frogs, geckos, skinks and beetles take refuge in cracks and crevices.

Echidna

Gecko

Koala

Praying mantid

63

INDEX

algae 45, 61
ambergris 6, 13
angler fish 24
ant 16, 18, 48
antenna 21, 48–49, 61
arachnids 49, 63
   mite 49
   tick 49
   scorpion 31, 49
   spider 25–27, 30–31, 49, 51
archer fish 24
arthropods 46, 49
azure kingfisher 55
baleen plate 14
bat 8, 10–11, 22–24, 32, 36, 63
beak 35
beetles 28, 49, 55, 63
birds 11, 16, 19, 25, 32–38, 40, 54, 62–63
biscuit sea star 58
black-footed rock wallaby 19
blowhole 15
blue-ringed octopus 31, 50, 58, 59
blue whale 12–13, 14
bolas spider 27
bombardier beetle 28
box jellyfish 24, 31, 58
boxer crab 28, 29
budgerigar 19
bull ant 48
butterfly 43–49
carnivore 11, 46
casque 38
cassowary 38
caterpillar 43–44, 47
cephalopods 4, 59, 61; see also cuttlefish, nautilus, octopus, squid
Christmas beetle 48
Christmas tree worm 58
cicada 44, 48, 62
cloaca 16
clownfish 58
cnidocytes 60–61
cnidarians 60; see also jellyfish, coral, sea anemone
cockatoo 32–34
cockroach 37, 44
cocoon 18, 45, 47
compound eyes 21, 49, 61
cone shell 4, 31
cone snail 31, 61
coral polyp 56–58, 60
cormorant 35
crocodile, estuarine 25, 40–41
crop, of bird 32
crow 35
crucifix frog 47
crustaceans 28, 45, 55, 58, 59, 61
lobster 45, 61
shrimp 14, 16, 18, 24, 28, 61
barnacle 45, 61
krill 15, 61
cuttlefish 13, 42–43, 61
damselfly 55
dingo 8, 19, 25
diving beetle 55
dolphin 8, 10, 12–15, 23–24

dragonfly 37, 44, 48, 55
duck 33, 35, 55
dugong 8, 13, 14, 58
dung beetle 48
dunnart 8
eastern brown snake 30, 31
echidna 8, 16–17, 63
echinoderms 61
echolocation 15, 22–23
ectothermic creatures 40
electroreception 16
emu 35, 38
exoskeleton 25, 49, 61
eyes 10–11, 16–17, 20–21, 24, 46, 49, 59
falcon 33, 35
fangs 26–27, 31, 41
feather-horned beetle see antenna
feet 35
fiddler crab 51
fish 4, 24, 29–31, 37, 58, 60–61
flying fish 29, 36
freshwater mussel 55
frilled lizard 40, 51
frog 4, 18, 25, 31, 40, 44–47, 55, 63
funnel-web spider 27, 31
fur seal 8
gizzard 32, 35
gliding possums 20–21, 36–37, 62–63
goanna 63
golden orb weaver 26
golden-tailed gecko 28–29
grebe 35
gudgeon 55
hairy sea urchin 58
harlequin beetle 49
herbivore 10, 61
Hercules moth 44–45
heron 35
hooded parrot 54
humpback whale 12, 14
huntsman spider 25
inland taipan 25, 30–31, 40
insects 4, 16, 20–22, 24–27, 31, 35, 37, 40, 42, 44–46, 48–49, 54–55, 63
invertebrates 4, 59–61
jacana 35
jellyfish 4, 24, 30–31, 58, 60–61
kangaroo 2, 4–5, 8–10, 19, 25, 41
keratin 16, 38
killer whale 15, 23
kingfisher 55, 62
koala 8, 10, 21, 63
krill 14–15, 61
leaf katydid 43
leafy sea dragon 42–43
leopard sea cucumber 58
lionfish 30, 58
lizard 18–19, 25, 28–29, 37, 39–40, 51, 63
long-horned beetle 49
longneck turtle 55
long-tailed planigale 8
magnificent riflebird 51
mallard duck 33, 55

mammals 4–5, 8–17, 21, 25, 31, 33, 40, 59
   monotremes 8, 16
   marsupials 8, 19–20
   placental mammals 8
   marine mammals 12–13
mammary glands 8, 14
manta ray 58
mantis shrimp 28
marine invertebrates 60–61
   coral 4, 56–61
   sponge 4, 60
   jellyfish 24, 30, 60
   squid 4, 13, 15, 37, 60–61
   starfish 60–61
   crab 28–29, 45, 49, 51, 60–61
   marine worm 60
marine molluscs 4, 16, 53, 55, 60–61
marine worm 60
marsupials 8, 19–20
marsupium 8
mayfly 37
meadow argus butterfly 43
metamorphosis 44–45, 49
   complete 45
   incomplete 44
mimesis 42
molluscs 4, 16, 53, 55, 61
   cephalopod 4, 59, 61
   nudibranch 58, 61
monotremes 8, 16
mosquito larva 55
moth 20–22, 27, 43–45
nasute 54
native bee 48
nautilus, chambered 53, 61
net-casting spider 27
nocturnal creatures 20–22, 47, 63
northern leaf-tailed gecko 42
nudibranch 58, 61
nymph 44–45, 49, 54
octopus 2, 4, 31, 50, 58–61
ommatidia 21, 49
omnivore 11
owl 20–21, 33, 62
oystercatcher 35
paper wasp 53
parrot 32, 35, 54
peacock spider 51
pheromones 21
pigeon 33
pink underwing moth caterpillar 43
pipit 35
platypus 8–9, 16–17
plover 29
pond snail 55
porpoise 12, 15, 23
possum 8–9, 20–21, 37, 41, 63
gliding possums 20–21, 36–37, 62–63
potoroo 9
praying mantid 48, 63
quoll 8, 11, 24
rainbowfish 55
raptor 35
ratites 38
red kangaroo 5, 9–10
red-tailed black cockatoo 32–33

redback spider 31
reef shark 58
reptiles 4, 16, 25, 31, 33, 40–41
rufous fantail 53
satin bower bird 52
scorpion 31, 49
scrub python 41
sea anemone 28–29, 60–61
sea lion 12–13
sea snail 61
sea slug see nudibranch 58, 61
sea snake 58, 61
seahorse 58
shield shrimp 18
skeleton 10–11, 49, 57, 61
snakes 2, 4, 20–21, 25, 30–31, 40–41
snipe 35
sperm whale 13, 15, 23
spiders 4, 25–27, 31, 49, 51
spinifex hopping mouse 19
spinneret 26, 49
spiracle 49
spoonbill 35
stingray 31
stonefish 30–31
sugar glider 20–21, 36–37, 62–63
tadpole 44–45, 55
tapetum lucidum 21
Tasmanian devil 8, 11, 24
tawny frogmouth 42
taxonomy 5
tegmina 37
termites 2, 16, 54, 63
thorny devil 18, 39
toothed whales 15
tree frog 47, 63
turtles 40–41, 55, 58
uterus 8
vertebrates 4–5, 46
vocal sac 47
water strider 55
water-holding frog 18
wedge-tailed eagle 62
whales 8, 12–15, 23–24, 45
willy wagtail 35
wings 11, 29, 32–38, 49
wombat 8
yabby 55
yellow-bellied glider 20–21

LEONARD CRONIN has been studying and writing about Australian wildlife for more than thirty years. Whether creating information books for children and adults, producing field guides, or writing articles for leading magazines, Leonard brings his own fascination with the natural world to the general reader. He lives and works in the hinterland of Byron Bay.

CHRIS NIXON is a visual artist based in Fremantle, creating across illustration, graphic design and public art installations. His work is inspired by nature and influenced by classic surf culture with an emphasis on the handmade and crafted, using colour, texture and pattern across a wide range of media. This book is the culmination of his passion for visual storytelling and his influences, for an exploration of the wild natural world in Australia.

First published by Allen & Unwin in 2022
Copyright © Text, Leonard Cronin 2022
Copyright © Illustrations, Chris Nixon 2022

All rights reserved. No part of this book may be reproduced or transmitted in any form or by any means, electronic or mechanical, including photocopying, recording or by any information storage and retrieval system, without prior permission in writing from the publisher. *The Australian Copyright Act 1968* (the Act) allows a maximum of one chapter or ten per cent of this book, whichever is the greater, to be photocopied by any educational institution for its educational purposes provided that the educational institution (or body that administers it) has given a remuneration notice to the Copyright Agency (Australia) under the Act.

Allen & Unwin
83 Alexander Street
Crows Nest NSW 2065
Australia
Phone: (61 2) 8425 0100
Email: info@allenandunwin.com
Web: www.allenandunwin.com

A catalogue record for this book is available from the National Library of Australia

ISBN 978 1 76063 722 4

For teaching resources, explore www.allenandunwin.com/resources/for-teachers

Illustrations were created with a blend of traditional and digital media: acrylic, ink and pencil, compiled and coloured in Photoshop and Illustrator.

Cover and text design by Kirby Armstrong
Set in 9.5 pt Futura

This book was printed in January 2022 by C&C Offset, China.

1 3 5 7 9 10 8 6 4 2

MIX
Paper from responsible sources
FSC® C008047